I0574009

The woman sitting next to me, noticing that my computer was closed, decided that it was okay to talk to me.

"Oh dear," she said. "I can't eat right now. Do you want this?" She held her plate out to me.

I instinctively leaned back, but there was nowhere to go. "No," I said, with my best polite, tight smile designed to be a friendly discouragement from interaction.

"Are you sure? I hate for it to go to waste. I paid extra for it."

"I can't," I said. "I'm allergic."

"Oh." The woman removed her plate from my face and set it back on her tray. "I'll have the young lady come and get it."

"That's not necessary," I said. "or really sa—"

The woman pressed the button.

"safe."

Didn't she realize that the flight attendant had to get up to come and see what the problem was? She was probably, most likely, buckled in herself, as she should be.

"Do you think she heard?" the woman asked, pressing the button again.

"I don't think it rings," I said. "I think it just lights up."

The flight attendant, holding onto the backs of the seats made her way toward our row.

"What can I get you Mrs. Evette?" she asked.

Mrs. Evette, my seat mate, held up her plate. "Would you

take this away." She lowered her voice to a stage whisper. "He's allergic."

Right now I was feeling allergic to people.

"Of course," the flight attendant said, taking the plate.

Just as she took the proffered plate, we hit another pocket of turbulence. It was almost like it was on cue.

The flight attendant held the plate close, and to avoid spilling the contents on me, she spilled it all over herself.

I looked up just as she looked at me.

She had the most beautiful green eyes I had ever seen. I would describe them as jade, like a mysterious mermaid haunting rocky shores. In that brief instant, I sensed happiness and positivity in a soul that ran deep.

As the plane dropped again, I instinctively reached out to keep her steady, breaking eye contact in the process.

Now that was smart. Now we both had short rib juice on us, though in all fairness, the flight attendant was the one who had taken the brunt.

It was all down the front of her uniform.

"Oh dear," my seat mate said.

The flight attendant smiled. She actually smiled.

ON THE EDGE OF CHANCE

ALSO BY KATHRYN KALEIGH

Contemporary Romance
The Worthington Family

The Lady in the Red Dress
On the Edge of Chance
Sealed with a Kiss
Billionaire's Unexpected Landing
Billionaire's Accidental Girlfriend
Billionaire Fallen Angel
Billionaire's Secret Crush
Billionaire's Barefoot Bride
The Heart of Christmas
The Magic of Christmas
In a One Horse Open Sleigh
A Secret Royal Christmas
An Old-Fashioned Christmas
Second Chance Kisses
Second Chance Secrets
First Time Charm
Three Broken Rules
Second Chance Destiny
Unexpected Vows
Begin Again
Love Again
Falling Again
Just Stay

Just Chance

Just Believe

Just Us

Just Once

Just Happened

Just Maybe

Just Pretend

Just Because

ON THE EDGE OF CHANCE

THE WORTHINGTONS

KATHRYN KALEIGH

ON THE EDGE OF CHANCE

SEALED WITH A KISS PREVIEW

Copyright © 2023 by Kathryn Kaleigh

All rights reserved.

Written by Kathryn Kaleigh.

Published by KST Publishing, Inc., 2023

Cover by Skyhouse24Media

www.kathrynkaleigh.com

No part of this book may be reproduced in any form or by any electronic or mechanical means, including information storage and retrieval systems, without written permission from the author, except for the use of brief quotations in a book review.

This is a work of fiction. Any names, characters, places, or incidents are products of the author's imagination and used in a fictitious manner. Any resemblance to actual people, places, of events is purely coincidental or fictionalized.

To learn more about Kathryn Kaleigh, visit

www.kathrynkaleigh.com

Kathryn Kaleigh

1

BROOKLYN JOHNSON

The weather in Houston was sunny and clear, not a cloud in the cerulean sky. A typical hot September day, temperatures bumping into the nineties.

The weather in Boston was cool and cloudy. We would be landing in Boston in approximately three hours and fifty minutes. An overnight trip for me.

Tomorrow I had a long day. A flight from Boston to Chicago. Then Chicago to Houston. But I would be back in my own place for the next three days after that.

The flight was crowded, every seat taken. Two hundred forty-two souls aboard including pilots and crew.

The coffee was brewed, ready to serve. The drink cart was ready the run through the coach section. Pretzels and peanuts.

First class passengers got four choices. Short ribs, rolls, and salad or tortellini and salad. Smoked salmon or a grain bowl. Personally, I preferred the tortellini with a side of tofu. Today's desert, all around, was a brownie with ice cream. Not bad for a four-hour commercial flight.

First class had sixteen passengers today. As for coach, I had just gotten back from a crosscheck of that section.

In row thirteen, a mother desperately tried to comfort her wailing infant.

In row three, three teenage boys slapped their hands together playing rock paper scissors.

In row twenty-three, a couple on their honeymoon seriously needed to get a room.

People who worked with me insisted that I had a super power.

I could remember everyone's seat and row number and something about them. It wasn't hard.

It actually felt like cheating, the way I did it. Row thirteen. Unlucky. Wailing infant. People would complain.

Row three. Three teens.

Row twenty-three. Well. It was hard to forget what I saw before I tossed a blanket over them. If I was any judge, the girl would be sleeping soundly for the duration of the flight.

"Prepare for takeoff."

The veteran pilot, Warren Adams, I'd flown with dozens of times, ran the words together so that they sounded like one word. Passengers would have no idea what he said.

I took my seat near the front of the jet and fastened my seatbelt. Warren was no-nonsense and expected his crew to be the same.

Friendly and efficient. That was our mission. And according to all accounts, I was the poster child.

"Hey," My friend and coworker, Lacy Montgomery, sat in the seat across from me and fastened her belt as the plane started moving.

"Hey." I said, with a smile.

"Did you see the guy in the fifth row?"

"The one with the beard?" I asked, wrinkling my nose.

"Oh. Right," she said. "I forgot. You don't like beards."

She was right. I had been raised around clean-shaven men. And since I came from a large family, that said a lot.

"I'm sure he's a perfectly nice guy," I said. "Why don't you ask him out?"

Lacy laughed. "You know me too well." Then she asked what she always asked. "If he has a friend, you want to come along?"

And I said what I always said. "I don't date passengers or pilots."

"You have too many rules," Lacy said, good-naturedly.

"Keeps me honest."

We stopped talking as the airplane left the ground, leaving nothing more than a pocket of air beneath us. The baby in row thirteen wailed louder, although how that was possible, I didn't really know.

"We're off," I said.

"You're lucky you have first class," Lacy said.

"I have confidence in your ability to take care of a crying baby."

Lacy rolled her eyes and unbuckled. "Wish me luck."

"Good luck," I said as Lacy headed toward coach.

I didn't leave my seat until the pilot gave the all clear signal.

I was like that. Rules were there for a reason, so unless I had a good reason to do otherwise, I followed them.

That gave me about another four minutes before I had to get to work. Whoever said first class was easier than coach had never worked first class. And today it was just me.

Two of the other flight attendants had called in sick, cutting us short. I didn't hold it against them. They were doing what they were told. Better that than bring something contagious onto a plane full of people.

And I secretly preferred to work my section alone. Even if it was a lot of work.

I was not afraid of hard work.

If there was nothing to do, I would find something.

That was how I had been raised.

The red light went off and I released my seatbelt.

Show time.

2

BENJAMIN GRAY

*I*t was a beautiful day for flying. A typical Wednesday. Clear blue skies.

Kids were back in school. Families were no longer on vacation.

We sat on the tarmac longer than usual, or at least it felt like it. And then we taxied forever. Maybe we were just going to drive to Boston.

I stuck my headphones into my ears, mostly to block out the sounds of a crying baby back in coach. I turned on some Frank Sinatra and closed my eyes. I used the time to think about my current project.

Once we were in the air, I could get some work done.

I had gotten myself into a bind with a deadline.

But my philosophy was family first.

And since my sister was having her first baby, it seemed like that should most definitely come first.

I could catch up on the work. I had no doubt about that. I just had to be left alone long enough. Sometimes I secured a private jet to take me across the country just to have a few hours of peace. I did some of my best writing in the air.

But since I had not been able to secure a private flight, I was stuck here in first class.

I usually flew with the private company, Skye Travels, but they had been booked up for today. I usually reserved ahead of time, but my sister's baby decided to come unexpectedly early.

Seemed like no matter how many pilots Noah Worthington hired, it was never enough.

Their reputation was stellar and they stayed booked out at least two weeks.

"Prepare for takeoff," the pilot announced over the speakers.

I was not a nervous flyer, but I did prefer to know who my pilot was. No reason. It was something I had gotten used to.

Reaching under my seat, I pulled out my laptop bag and powered on my computer.

I had a good, firm outline of my latest mystery novel, so all I had to do was to write the first draft. Second drafts were always easier because I had more of the idea down on my computer.

I was still on chapter one.

I lowered the volume on my headphones and pulled up my outline. The roar of the plane blocked out most of the background noise so it didn't take me long to get focused.

The passenger—an elderly well-dressed woman—sitting next to me tapped me on the shoulder.

"What are you doing?" she asked. "Are you working?"

"Yes," I said, trying not to sound annoyed.

"Are you going to Boston for work?"

"Yes," I said again, with a tight, forced smile. Actually the true answer was no. I was headed to Boston to be with my sister as she gave birth to her first child, but I certainly did not want to tell the woman that.

Babies were one of those topics one did not dare bring up with women. It tapped into their subconscious and they wanted to know everything.

She asked me something else, but pretending not to hear, I pointed to my headphones and shook my head. "Work," I said.

That usually did the trick. It was kind of funny. If people thought I was "working," they respected my time. If they somehow found out I was writing a novel, they thought it was okay to talk to me. Like writing wasn't "real work."

So I never purposely told anyone I was an author.

My seat mate looked disappointed that I didn't want to strike up a conversation, but it was better to disappoint her now than after I had wasted two hours of writing time.

Out of the corner of my eyes, I watched one of the uniformed flight attendants stopping at each aisle, taking drink orders. We had to pick our food orders at the time of ticket purchase, so there was no need to be bothered by that. And the thing about first class was the flight attendants didn't bother us until we wanted to be bothered.

So I kept my head down and my focus on the words on my screen. I was making some progress when it came time for the meals.

Unfortunately, the woman sitting next to me ordered the short ribs.

The flight attendant was careful not to disturb me as she handed over the plate. Even so, I caught a good whiff of the meat. I had to close my eyes and think about kittens chasing butterflies in a field to keep from gagging.

As a vegetarian, the scent of the short rib was enough to send me over the edge.

I couldn't blame anyone other than myself. I was the one who had chosen an aisle seat. I did not like to be cramped in, even if the view was better inside.

Just another reason to fly private.

On a private jet, there were no seat mates who ordered meat or asked pesky questions. It was just me and my own little world in the sky.

The fasten seatbelt light came on. I kept my seatbelt on. No reason not to. I was just sitting here anyway.

The pilot must have had some warning about impending turbulence.

The plane dropped, probably two feet, causing a lot of frightened gasps.

If I could, I would have told them that turbulence wasn't really dangerous. That it was to be expected and we would get through it just fine.

But even with my headphones in my ears, it was hard to concentrate, so I pulled them out and closed my computer.

I rested my hands on the computer and waited for the commotion to die down.

Instead, we hit another pocket.

The woman sitting next to me, noticing that my computer was closed, decided that it was okay to talk to me.

"Oh dear," she said. "I can't eat right now. Do you want this?" She held her plate out to me.

I instinctively leaned back, but there was nowhere to go. "No," I said, with my best polite, tight smile designed to be a friendly discouragement from interaction.

"Are you sure? I hate for it to go to waste. I paid extra for it."

"I can't," I said. "I'm allergic."

"Oh." The woman removed her plate from my face and set it back on her tray. "I'll have the young lady come and get it."

"That's not necessary," I said. "or really sa—"

The woman pressed the button.

"safe."

Didn't she realize that the flight attendant had to get up to come and see what the problem was? She was probably, most likely, buckled in herself, as she should be.

"Do you think she heard?" the woman asked, pressing the button again.

"I don't think it rings," I said. "I think it just lights up."

The flight attendant, holding onto the backs of the seats made her way toward our row.

"What can I get you Mrs. Evette?" she asked.

Mrs. Evette, my seat mate, held up her plate. "Would you take this away." She lowered her voice to a stage whisper. "He's allergic."

Right now I was feeling allergic to people.

"Of course," the flight attendant said, taking the plate.

Just as she took the proffered plate, we hit another pocket of turbulence. It was almost like it was on cue.

The flight attendant held the plate close, and to avoid spilling the contents on me, she spilled it all over herself.

I looked up just as she looked at me.

She had the most beautiful green eyes I had ever seen. I would describe them as jade, like a mysterious mermaid haunting rocky shores. In that brief instant, I sensed happiness and positivity in a soul that ran deep.

As the plane dropped again, I instinctively reached out to keep her steady, breaking eye contact in the process.

Now that was smart. Now we both had short rib juice on us, though in all fairness, the flight attendant was the one who had taken the brunt.

It was all down the front of her uniform.

"Oh dear," my seat mate said.

The flight attendant smiled. She actually smiled.

"It's okay," she said. "Don't worry. I'll get this cleaned up."

I released my hold on her and she turned, taking the offending plate, practically empty now, with her. The food was on the floor in the aisle next to my seat.

Mrs. Evette pulled napkins out of somewhere and, leaning over me, attempted to begin cleaning up the mess on the arm of my seat.

"Please," I said, taking the napkins from her. "Let me do it."

Kleenex, the woman was using Kleenex and I was making

an even bigger mess with them, but the flight attendant was already back with a bucket and a rag. She had the mess cleaned up in no time flat.

She must do this a lot, I thought absently.

"I'm so sorry this happened," she said to me. "Can I get you anything?"

"No," I said. "Please. Sit. Until we get through this turbulence."

"I'll be back," she said and disappeared.

I leaned my head back and tried to breathe through my mouth. Was it really necessary for people to eat on airplanes? Couldn't they just wait until they got where they were going?

Maybe this was why I wrote murder mysteries. It was my way of getting rid of offending people. A socially acceptable way of turning them into a character and killing them off.

About twenty minutes later, with no more turbulence, the red light went off.

The flight attendant came back as promised.

She handed me a drink. A vodka martini, dirty.

"How did you know to bring this?" I asked. "That I like these?"

"It was on your profile," she said. She had changed her uniform. I didn't even want to think about how that might have happened. The little bathrooms, even in first class, were barely enough to stand in.

"Right. I suppose it was." I didn't remember putting that on anything when I bought the ticket. The questions they did ask were optional, but I answered them anyway, mostly out of curiosity.

On occasion I drank a vodka martini when I flew with Skye Travels, but rarely.

Their databases didn't connect. Did they?

"Would you like your tortellini now?" she asked, with that same pleasant smile.

"That would be nice. Thank you." I really didn't want it. I only wanted it because she offered it. Good thing she didn't offer me something with beef in it. I just might have taken it.

There were some rules a man had to break and right now vegetarianism seemed like one of those breakable rules.

Apparently, since I had what they called short ribs on my tie, I was going to be smelling it all the way to Boston. What was the difference in that and eating it, really?

A few minutes later, the flight attendant brought my plate, vegetarian tortellini, and set it on the tray in front of me.

"Thank you," I said.

"Oh that looks so good," Mrs. Evette said. "So much better than what I ordered."

I sighed. Then did what any gentleman would do.

I handed it over to her. "Please," I said. "Take mine."

"Oh no," Mrs. Evette said. "I couldn't possibly."

"Of course, you can," I said. "Remember," I tapped my computer. "I have work to do."

She took the plate from me and happily munched on it while I happily tapped away on my computer keys.

It was a match made in heaven.

3

BROOKLYN

I fastened my seatbelt and prepared for landing. I was exhausted—in a good way. It was my job to keep the passengers under my watch safe and happy. So that's what I did.

I considered myself a complicated person. I came by that naturally. Both my mother and my grandmother were psychologists. That in itself was enough to mess someone up.

Then there was my grandfather, Noah Worthington. Grandpa Noah had built a private airline company, starting with one airplane, into a multi-billionaire dollar private airline company. Grandpa Noah was a legend in aviation.

Newly graduating pilots aspired to work at Skye Travels more than the big commercial airlines. Skye Travels was considered a prestigious and elite place to work.

I had a lot of entrepreneurial blood running through my veins. But for me, it was like a recessive gene. I loved learning though. I'd graduated from Harvard with a degree in business. I'd been offered some enviable jobs in big companies. And, one by one, I had turned them down.

There was also Skye Travels. I could have worked there as a Vice-President if I wanted to. But I had stayed away from that, too.

I wanted to be my own person. Even so, I didn't stray far from the family business. I'd grown up around airplanes. Grandpa had me in the cockpit of a Cessna before I could walk. I had the photo to prove it. I suppose flying ran through my blood like jet fuel.

I'd gotten some of my mother and grandmother's blood, too. I like people. But I didn't want to sit with them and listen to their problems. I liked happy people.

So I had put those two things together and became a flight attendant. Personally, I preferred the title stewardess. I knew my history. The term steward was used in the early days of ocean travel. And since I didn't mind people calling me a girl or a lady, why would I be offended by the term stewardess?

At any rate, I kept that particular thought to myself. I did not care to have rocks thrown at me.

I had some clear-cut rules about my life that I followed. Such as not dating pilots or passengers. Such as following the pilot's directions about when to stay seated and when it was okay to move about.

But I broke my rules when I needed to. I figured since I had made the rules, I decided when to break them. There were no police with flashing lights in my head to give me tickets when I broke one of my rules.

I had broken two rules on this particular flight.

One, I had moved about when Mrs. Evette turned on her call button. She was an older woman, traveling alone, so it was quite possible that she really needed something. That had gone badly and had reminded me why I had rules. Actually the seat belt rule was someone else's, so I only had myself to blame.

All Mrs. Evette wanted was for me to take her plate. Which

I did. All over my uniform. I had quickly cleaned it up, only because the man sitting next to her, Benjamin Gray, looked like he was going to be sick.

I shuddered to think what might have happened if he hadn't caught me when that last turbulence hit. I could have been injured. Again, rules were there for a reason.

Benjamin had blue eyes that reminded me of a clear sky with tiny little shards of violet that one wouldn't notice unless they were just inches away.

At any rate, since he had saved me, I wanted to do something nice for him. That led to me breaking a second rule.

It was a rule I rarely broke, but this seemed like a fitting occasion for it.

Like all the Worthington teenagers, I had worked at Skye Travels during my summer breaks. My job had been in scheduling. And when needed, I could still fill in.

Using my access, I logged into the Skye Travels website to see if he had an account. I had no reason to think that he might. It was just a lucky guess. Maybe a gut feeling.

And... he did. Benjamin Gray was a frequent flyer with Skye Travels.

It had been a pleasant surprise to see that I had been right. It was possible I had seen him or maybe his name before.

Benjamin had a Houston address. Made sense. A quick scan of his flight records told me he had never flown to Boston on a Skye Travels flight.

He didn't make a lot of requests. A very low maintenance traveler. But according to his account, he did like vodka martinis.

As we went in for a landing, I realized that I may have tipped my hand, so to speak. I'd done something that I wasn't supposed to do. And now he would always wonder how I just so happened to pick his favorite drink.

Well, I decided, as the pilot began to taxi down the runway, life was much more interesting when there a few little unexplained mysteries now and then.

4

BENJAMIN

*M*y sister, Analise, sat propped against pillows in the hospital bed. Her large private room was overflowing with brightly colored flowers, balloons, and teddy bears.

"You look like hell," I said.

"Thank you," she said, looking down at the twin girls she had given birth to merely hours ago. Fortunately, she'd gotten the birthing over with before I got there.

"What are you going to do with two girls?" I asked, sitting on the edge of her bed.

Analise and I were kindred spirits in many ways. I think she could have gone through life without children, but she loved her husband dearly. Enough to traumatize her body by birthing twins.

She shrugged.

"Did you know you were having twins?"

She wrinkled her nose. "The doctor might have mentioned it."

I laughed. "It's kind of a big thing."

She looked up at me then and I saw desperation in her eyes.

"We should talk before Robert gets back."

"Talk about what?" I asked with alarm. "Please don't tell me you're getting divorced." Not with two babies. Our parents would have to become parents all over again.

"After this? No way. He's tethered to me for life."

"A brutal image." But one that came with relief.

She was still attached to monitors and one of them was beeping.

"Do I need to get a nurse?" I asked.

"No," she said. "They just show up."

Right on cue, a nurse made an obligatory knock before stepping inside. She carried a bag of fluid.

"See," Analise said with a flourish of her hand.

I nodded and watched as the nurse deftly changed out the empty bag of fluid for a full one.

"Feeling okay?" the nurse asked.

Analise made a face. The nurse just laughed. "It gets better."

"It has to get better," Analise muttered under her breath.

The nurse left us alone again.

"What did you want to tell me?"

"Oh. Right." She lowered her voice to a whisper. "I was thinking. Since there are two of them." She glanced at the twins in her arms. "You can take one for yourself."

It took me a minute to absorb what she was saying, but when I did, I laughed.

"How much dope did they give you?"

"Not enough." She pushed out her bottom lip.

"What about Robert? Think he would go for your plan? He was looking awfully proud when he walked out of here.

"Maybe he won't remember there were two of them. I'll convince him he was seeing double."

"I think you're insane," I said. "And anyway, what would I do with a baby?"

She waved a hand and closed her eyes. "You're a writer, you have plenty of time."

"My own sister," I muttered.

She opened one eye and looked at me. "When are you going to get married already? Make your own babies?"

"It's kinda hard to get married when I'm not dating anyone."

"You stay to yourself too much," she said, shifting a bit. Nothing I hadn't heard before. "Here hold a baby." Now that was something I had not heard before.

"I don't—" But she was already lifting one of them.

I took the baby and held it at arm's length.

"Hold her close," Analise said. "Like this." She cradled the other one to her.

With a glare at my sister, I held the baby to me and looked down at her.

"She's kind of cute," I said.

"Of course she is. She came out of this." She swept a hand in the general direction of her body.

"There's something wrong with you," I said.

"Probably," she said, shoving her hair back.

"She smiled at me," I said, with a quick glance in my sister's direction.

"She can't smile. She's two minutes old."

"She smiled," I said.

"Okay. That settles it. You take that one."

"Thanks," I said. "I'm going to name her… Brooklyn."

5

BROOKLYN

*M*y flight was cancelled.

It stormed the entire next day, leaving thousands of travelers stranded.

Luckily, I spent the day in my perfectly nice hotel room, monitoring the weather and my phone apps.

No planes were leaving and none were coming in. The day of storms was going to disrupt flights for days.

By the next morning, the weather was clear, but trees limbs and fallen debris were scattered everywhere.

I stayed in my room until eleven o'clock before I called an Uber to take me to the airport.

We drove past the terminal gates, lines backed up all over the place and went straight to the private terminal.

I had nothing in Boston. No reason to stay here. I could walk around the Harvard campus and revisit my old haunts, but I didn't have the inclination for reminiscing at the moment.

So I'd done what anyone in my shoes would do. I called my Grandpa.

A Phenom with the Skye Travels logo was sitting there on the tarmac by the time I got to the terminal.

I walked straight through to the tarmac.

Grandpa was standing outside the airplane waiting for me.

"Hey Kitten," he said and hugged me.

"Thank you for coming to get me."

"It's no big deal. I had to come this way anyway to pick up another passenger. So you'll have company on the flight."

"Okay," I said. "I don't mind."

"I didn't think you would."

He took my luggage.

"Want me to get that?" I asked.

"I'm not an old man yet," Grandpa Noah said. "I can still handle a girl's luggage."

I sighed. Of course he could. Grandpa Noah still looked as strong as ever, but he was pushing seventy. He carried it well. Silver hair beneath his dashing captain's hat. The same charming grin I'd seen in photographs of him and Grandma back when they were younger.

"You ready?" he asked after stashing my luggage.

"When you are."

I went up the stairs first, with him behind me.

"I brought Cody," Grandpa said behind me. No school today.

"Oh. Okay." I wouldn't be sitting in the cockpit. Cody was my little brother. There were five of us siblings. Two boys with three girls in the middle. Grandpa often brought one his grandchildren with him when he flew.

Just inside the plane, I froze.

"You okay?" Grandpa asked.

"Sorry." I stepped inside, realizing I'd left him standing on the stairs.

Benjamin sat in one of the black leather seats.

He looked up and his shocked gaze mirrored mine.

"Benjamin," Grandpa said. "This is Brooklyn."

Neither one of us said anything.

"You two know each other?" Grandpa asked, stepping past me to the cockpit.

"No."

"Yes."

"Yes."

"No."

"Well, Grandpa said. "Sit wherever you like."

He stepped into the cockpit, leaving us.

"How are you here?" he asked.

"How are you here?" I answered.

He closed his computer and looked at me. I sat down across from him. He spoke first.

"I had to leave before my sister forced me to take one of her newborn twins."

"What?" I asked. "Your sister tried to give you a baby?"

He shrugged. "You'd have to know my sister."

"Sounds like you have an interesting family." I pulled my purse off over my head and set it on the seat next to me. "You haven't seen her lately?"

I realized I shouldn't be asking this before I even finished the sentence. I knew that he hadn't been to Boston on Skye Travels. But there were other airlines.

"I saw them last year over the holidays. They just moved from Denver."

"Ah." I had seen Denver on his flight log. Several times. It wasn't my fault I had a good memory.

"But you," he said. "What are you doing here?"

"There were no flights out yesterday."

"The storm."

"So everything is backed up. It'll take days to sort everything out."

"I can imagine." He looked at me, waiting for me to say more.

I had evaded his question.

"Fasten your seat belts." Grandpa said.

Benjamin was already buckled in. I checked. I couldn't help it. It was ingrained in me.

I secured my own seatbelt and settled into my seat.

"I would think they would need you on one of the flights," he said, not letting it go.

"It's my day off," I said with a little smile.

"Okay," he said. "Maybe you'll tell me later."

"Maybe," I said, biting my lip and looking up at him from beneath my lashes.

He just smiled at me.

"I won't bother you," I said, sitting back in my seat and closing my eyes as Grandpa took the airplane up.

6

BENJAMIN

I had flown with Noah Worthington once before. It was his company. He created it and he grew it into an empire.

He hired his family and he never tried to hide it. But he never hired anyone in his family until they were ready. The word was that he was actually harder on his family members than he was with the other people he hired.

Noah took the airplane up without a hitch. I pretended to look out the window until we hit cruising altitude.

I quietly tapped the top of my closed laptop.

This was my prime writing time.

The roar of the engine. The freedom of isolation. Being up here in my own little world.

Most writers, they say, have some kind of eccentricity. Maybe this was mine.

There was just one problem.

First of all, I'd always flown alone when I flew Skye Travels. It messed up my concentration to have someone else in my cabin.

Second. It was her. Brooklyn.

I only knew her name because I'd heard one of the other flight attendants call her name. After our encounter with the turbulence and the short ribs, I'd started paying attention.

Try as I might, I couldn't make the pieces fit together.

And as a mystery writer, I couldn't not try to solve a mystery.

Brooklyn was a mystery. Somehow she had known my favorite drink—a dirty vodka martini, and now she was on my private flight back to Houston.

Noah had not said anything to me about it. I had assumed he was checking the airplane or some such when he was outside. I hadn't known that he waiting for another passenger.

If it had been anyone other than Brooklyn, I would have been more than a little unhappy.

As it was, this was like some kind of fortuitous hand of fate.

I'd been thinking about her for two days now. I'd even suggested that my sister name her child after her.

The damnedest thing was that Analise had done it. She had named one of them Brooklyn and the other one Savannah. I understood Savannah. We had been born and bred there.

I hadn't really meant for her to name her child after a woman I would never see again.

But here she was. Right here on my privately chartered jet.

When she pulled a novel out of her handbag and started reading, I knew I was in love.

I watched her out of the corner of my eye. Everything about her was perfect. She had a lean, healthy build and was about a head shorter than me. Her softly curled brunette hair fell over her shoulders. I hadn't known that before because she'd had it pulled back.

Her bow shaped lips were slightly parted as she read, her brow furrowed in concentration.

I wanted to ask her what she was reading. I wanted to talk to her.

But I could not in good conscience interrupt her when being interrupted was the thing I disliked most having done to me.

So finally, after she turned a page in her book, I opened my laptop and forced myself to concentrate on my own story.

After a few minutes, we fell into a companionable silence and I actually got another chapter written.

But even as I was writing, I was thinking about Brooklyn. Wondering how she was here. Where was she going? And how did she end up on my airplane?

7

BROOKLYN

*I*t was hard to read with Benjamin watching me. I pretended not to notice.

But I was relieved when he finally opened his computer and started working.

Countless people got work done while they flew on Skye Travels private jets. The bulk of our passengers were people traveling for work. We occasionally got honeymooners or others who wanted to fly private for other reasons.

My Aunt Ainsley had started her own division flying seeing-eye dogs for people. It was a surprisingly large neglected market when she started doing it.

I was curious about what, exactly, Benjamin was doing. He typed fast, whatever it was.

I had reflexively hedged when he'd asked me what I was doing on his airplane. He hadn't used those words, but I suspected that was what he was thinking. It would be what I was thinking if I were in his shoes.

Having another passenger along wasn't part of the deal.

People paid for private jets. And private meant that there were no other passengers.

I probably should have just told him.

That's Noah Worthington, owner and founder of Skye Travels and I'm his granddaughter. I didn't want to wait for a commercial seat on a commercial airline—the airline that employees me. That's why I got to crash—bad choice of words—intrude—upon your private flight.

I didn't tell people that I was a Worthington for a reason. Not technically a Worthington, but my mother was a Worthington so I was half Worthington. At any rate, I didn't want people to think I was getting special treatment.

But the thing was, sometimes I did get special treatment. Like today. Everyone else had to wait for a seat to get where they were going. Some people even had emergencies and had to wait.

And even though it would be nice to be able to help all of them get where they were going, I couldn't.

And since it wasn't possible, I dealt with it by telling people who I was on a need to know basis.

I would tell Benjamin. It was only fair. And I would request that he be given a discount on his next flight with us.

It was the right thing to do.

And all that was just the business side of things.

There was a whole other side.

I *liked* him. I liked the way he looked at me with his deep blue eyes. Eyes that reminded me of those tiny little wild blue daisies that sprouted up every spring in my parents' back yard. When those daisies came out, I knew Spring was here. And I always picked one. Just one. In celebration of the start of my favorite time of year.

He was clean-shaven just like I liked my men. A strong jaw. He was lean and just the right height.

I couldn't find anything I didn't like about him except that he was a passenger. And now that I knew he was a Skye Travels passenger, it went even more against the rules I had set for myself to get to know him on a personal level. A dating level.

It had been a really long time since I had found someone I was interested in dating. Since I was only around passengers, I didn't really get the chance to meet very many other people.

I was definitely an anomaly in the flight attendant world. Like my friend, Lacy, most flight attendants purposefully made it a point seek out people to date that they met on the airplanes. A dating pool. But for me, passengers were not a dating pool.

But as I sat trying to read, with Benjamin halfway working and halfway studying me, I wondered. I wondered what if...

8

BENJAMIN

*A*s the airplane began its initial descent into Houston, I put my computer away and Brooklyn put her book away.

"What are you reading?" I asked, finally feeling like I could ask.

"It's sort of a mystery novel. Mystery and romance."

"My favorite," I said. That was exactly what I wrote.

"You sound like you're writing a book over there."

"You have experience with writers?"

"I've had a few passengers who were writers."

"I see." I stretched out my legs. "I have a proposition for you."

"A proposition?"

"Yes. When you tell me how you ended up on this airplane, I'll tell you what I'm working on."

She smiled. Brooklyn had one of those smiles that men would go to war over.

"Deal," she said, holding out a hand to shake mine.

I took her hand, but somehow the intent of a handshake was lost in translation.

We were going in for a landing now, trees and buildings whipping past outside the windows and I found myself holding her hand.

She didn't try to pull away, but I saw something change in her eyes. An awareness and an attraction.

"There is one problem with your proposition," she said as the wheels hit the runway.

"What's that?" I was tamping down a sense of panic. Not from flying, but from knowing that she and I were about to part ways. And we were still no more than strangers on a plane.

"The problem is that even though we've encountered each other twice, by chance, we're not likely to encounter each other again."

I nodded and tried not to smile. "You said that much better than I could have."

"I doubt that."

She looked at me with her head tilted slightly to one side.

"Let me amend my proposition," I said.

"We have about five minutes."

"I'll talk fast."

She smiled.

"Are you familiar with the Sky House Restaurant across the freeway from the airport?"

"I am."

"We could have a drink and sort all this out."

She looked past me out the window.

"Seems only fair. Since I hijacked your flight, that you hijack my ride."

"Is that your car?" I asked following her gaze.

"Probably."

"The plot thickens, as they say."

"I guess we have a plan, then."

"I guess so."

"Benjamin?"

"Yes?"

"I'm gonna need my hand back."

"Right." I released her hand. I hadn't forgotten I was holding it. On the contrary, it felt perfectly normal.

I was elated knowing that I was going to get to spend a bit more time with her, to get to know more about her.

Happy. That was what I was going with. For now, at least.

9

BROOKLYN

*A*s Grandpa taxied the plane along the runway up to our terminal, Benjamin held my hand. It was supposed to have been a handshake, but it had turned into something else.

It had turned into handholding.

It occurred to me that I was about to break another rule.

As Grandpa secured the plane and I gathered up my things, I realized that I *wanted* to break my rule about not dating passengers. Granted a drink was not a date. Exactly. But it felt like a date.

And I was going to call it a date, whether Benjamin did or not.

I had learned somewhere along the way that I could call things whatever I wanted. Nobody really cared.

And calling things what it suited me to call them, in my head at least, kept me content with my life.

My family was used to me using my own language. When I talked to them, I was a stewardess and no one minded.

I loved having a family who accepted me for who I was and not for who they wanted me to be.

When I was younger, in college even, I hadn't been sure that was going to be how it was. All my cousins and even my older brother fell into the family business. Not only without question, but with what I called eagerness. They were all eager to jump into something that had already been decided for them.

So I went my own way. I know they didn't understand why I was using my college degree from Harvard to work as a stewardess. But they let me be.

Grandpa came out of the cockpit, my little brother behind him.

Cody looked at Benjamin and just nodded in greeting to both of us. Grandpa lowered the stairs and went down first. At the bottom of the stairs, he was there to help us as needed.

"Is that my car?" I asked Grandpa as I stepped onto the ground.

"I think so."

"Thank you," I said.

"Don't mention it."

I reached the limo driver, Peter, who'd been with the family for years.

"Would you take us to the Sky House across the street?" I asked.

"Of course, Miss Brooklyn."

Since he called me by my first name, I didn't have to worry about him giving away my identity.

He opened the back door and I slid inside. A couple of minutes later, Benjamin got in on the other side.

As we settled into the back seat of the car, the driver put our luggage in the trunk.

"Do you have a car here?" I asked, mostly just to make conversation.

"It's in the covered parking area. You?"

I smiled just a little. "No."

This little caper of ours might just be fun.

10

BENJAMIN

I would come back for my car. It wasn't a big deal.

It was a big deal that Brooklyn had a car waiting for her when we landed at the airport.

Again, something did not add up with her.

She was a flight attendant who flew in private jets on her own time?

It only took a few minutes to get across the freeway. The driver pulled up to the door of the Sky House, not related or to be confused with Skye Travels.

I was surprised that Noah Worthington hadn't tried to incorporate it into his company. I'd asked one of the pilots once about it. The answer was something vague about Noah not wanting to get into the food and drink industry.

He'd probably considered it. But he was a smart man. If he didn't go in a direction, he had a good reason.

It was a bit unsettling sitting this close to Brooklyn. We were close enough that I could put my arm around her, but that would have been a cliched high school boy move.

As it was, we rode in silence to the Sky House.

When the limo driver pulled up to the front, he parked and

opened Brooklyn's door for her. I could have done that. Would have done it.

But she met me on my side with a smile.

The concierge opened the door to the restaurant and we walked into the crowded restaurant. Only a few tables were available, from what I could see.

"Would you like your usual booth, Miss Brooklyn?" one of two young female hostesses asked.

"Yes, please," Brooklyn said with a little smile.

She glanced at me before we followed the hostess to a booth in the back of the restaurant.

I grinned. Another mysterious clue about her. For the hostess to know her and for her to have "a usual" table, I could safely say that Brooklyn came here often.

We sat across from each other in a cozy little booth in the back of the restaurant. Barely discernible music played over the speakers. Eighties music, I decided, catching just a hint here and there.

Several tables had been pushed together in the middle of the room for a party. Looked like a bridal shower. And the young ladies were giggling like teenagers.

I couldn't help but think of my sister. She was on the other side of the whole bridal shower thing. It was all fun and games until you went home with twin girls.

A server stopped at our table before we had time to settle in good.

"Hi Aaron," Brooklyn said.

"Hello Miss Brooklyn. "Your martini is on the way." He looked at me. "What can I get you Sir?

"A martini for me, too, please."

From where I was sitting, this changed things a little bit.

I had thought that Brooklyn knew what my drink of choice was. It could be that it she chose it for me on plane because it was her favorite drink. So I took a step back on that one and gave her the benefit of the doubt.

There was still the fact that she had ended up on my airplane, rode in a chauffeured car, and was a regular here, at the Sky House. Not the usual things for a stewardess... flight attendant.

Those were things to be explored for an explanation.

"Where were we?" she asked.

"We were figuring out that people here seem to know you."

"I live in Houston," she said.

Alright. Since she gave me one, I'd give her one back.

"I live in Houston, too."

She smiled at me, but it was a secretive smile. One that made me think maybe she already knew this.

"How does this work?" I asked.

"You tell me. It was your proposition."

So it was.

"How about we both get three questions." I said.

The server brought our martinis.

I lifted my glass.

"To life's mysteries."

11

BROOKLYN

"*T*hree questions, huh?"

Benjamin had no idea how many skills I had. After all, my mother and my grandmother were both psychologists. I knew a thing or two about people.

He nodded once, not trying to talk over the burst of laughter coming from the bridal shower.

"Deal," I said. I wouldn't need three questions, but I'd take them as a token of good sportsmanship. "I'll even let you go first."

"Okay," he leaned forward.

"But," I held up a finger. "There are rules to this game."

"What kind of rules?" he sat back.

"You can't ask direct questions about the topic of discussion."

"I don't know this game."

I grinned. "Then I guess I have a slight home field advantage."

"And yet I'm from here, too."

I shrugged and looked at him as I took a sip of my drink.

"Feel free to withdraw from the game at any time."

He laughed. "Not a chance."

"Do you want me to go first?"

"You have to give a guy time to form his strategy."

"You're a chess player," I said.

"That's not a question."

"It's just an observation," I said, warming to the game. "And it's not my turn anyway."

"Where did you go to college?" he asked.

I used my lips to slip an olive off the toothpick. He seemed a little distracted by that as I had intended.

"Harvard." Now he was even more confused.

If he could figure me out, he was a better man than most.

"My turn. You have one sister. Older than you."

"How do you know that?

I would never try to give my older brother one of my babies, but with my younger brother, all bets were off.

"I haven't asked my question yet."

"Okay." He leaned back and loosened his tie a bit. He was studying me again in that way that gave me goosebumps.

"What was your college major?" I asked.

"Business. Good question."

I smiled. Knowing his major potentially gave me more information than where he went to school. For the most part.

"Who do you live with?"

Impressive. He was cutting to the chase.

"I live alone. Would you rather spend a Sunday afternoon at a baseball game with the guys or with family?"

"What does that—" He stopped himself and shook his head. "Family."

"You get one more question."

He turned his drink by the stem. "I think I'll save my question."

"I'm not sure that's legal."

He laughed. "Didn't you make the rules?"

I nodded. "I did. And I decide what's legal."

"Then you let me know when you figure out whether or not a question can be held until later."

"I have to think about it," I said. "Okay. It's legal."

"That was fast."

"I don't play."

"Too bad," he said, sitting back in the booth.

Too bad, indeed.

I wondered if he was thinking what I was thinking.

12

BENJAMIN

I had no doubt that Brooklyn was better at this game than I was. It was, after all, her game.

I was better at solving mysteries in my books than I was at trying to figure out a real person.

Brooklyn was most definitely a real person.

The way she slid her olives off her toothpicks had me thinking things that I would imagine she would find inappropriate. I could be wrong about her, but my impression of her was that she was a refined, classy lady.

I had already formed an impression of what she was like and yet I had more questions than answers.

But I had a strategy.

She had been right about me being a chess player. She had also been right about me having an older sister. She didn't know that I had an older brother, too, but that was a story for a different time.

My strategy was to get her talking. I could find out more about her from her talking than I could from trying to figure out which questions to ask her.

"I don't think I've ever seen this place this crowded," I said.

She scanned the room. "It's pretty crowded. It gets this way, especially on the weekends. During the week, especially at lunch, there usually aren't that many people in here."

"It's still fairly early, too."

"This is true."

I had a feeling Brooklyn was allowing me clues without me asking. But I didn't mind. I just liked talking with her.

"Can I ask you something unrelated?" I asked.

"Sure."

"Do you think the Houston Astros are going to take the World Series championship again?"

"Of course I do," she said with a little laugh. "I wouldn't be a born and bred Houstonian if I didn't."

"Right." And, of course, being from Savannah, I could not completely understand that at the level she did.

She sat back and snagged my gaze. "So tell me what you have so far."

"On you?"

"Of course."

"You're a beautiful young lady from Houston, Texas. Optimistic and friendly. Kind. A competent and caring flight attendant." He looked at me quizzically. "I still don't understand how you came to be on my airplane. I don't think the airline would pay for you to fly private."

I shook my head in agreement. "Doesn't seem likely, does it?"

She wasn't wearing her uniform and her hair was down. And yet I had recognized her instantly.

"Let me see your shoes," I said.

"My shoes?"

"Yes. Come on." I patted the seat next to me. "Shoes."

"Why?" she asked on a little bubble of laughter.

"I think I have it figured out."

She complied and put her feet on the edge of the seat next to me.

"Yep," I said after one look. "I'm beginning to see how you ended up on my airplane."

13

BROOKLYN

*A*s the voices got louder in the restaurant, it seemed like the music got louder along with it. There was also a television on over at the bar and a group of men had gathered around to watch it. A football game from the sounds of it.

I couldn't help but wonder if they had been drawn here because of the bridal shower since bridal showers tended to attract single women.

Aaron stopped by to take our order. I ordered some cheese sticks for an appetizer and a shrimp salad for my meal. Benjamin ordered a hamburger and French fries.

Since it was comfortable, I kept my feet propped on Benjamin's side of the booth. He didn't seem to mind and he'd started it, after all.

"Are you going to tell me what you think you have figured out?" I asked, after Aaron left us alone again.

"You're a widow with a small child at home. Your husband left you enough money to make you independently wealthy. You work as a part time flight attendant to keep yourself from going stir crazy and because you like to travel on occasion."

I was speechless. "Wow." It was the only word I could come up with in the moment.

"Am I right?" he asked, smiling.

"How is it that my husband passed away?" I asked, avoiding his question.

"He had taken his sailboat out for a spin in Boston harbor and a sudden storm blew up. Without any warning. Nothing in the forecast. He was swept away. After an extensive search, his body was never found, but the boat washed ashore several miles up north. You sold the house you had in Boston. It was too big and lonely. And you moved home to a smaller, more manageable condo here to be near your family."

I put a hand over my mouth to keep from laughing. But Benjamin looked serious.

"That's quite a backstory you've invented for me."

"I'm right, aren't I?"

"Let me see. I've never been married. But I do like to travel on occasion."

How could I not like to travel? Traveling was in my blood. It ran right alongside the jet fuel. In fact, it was fueled by the jet fuel in my veins.

He leaned back. Put a hand on one of my shoes. It was an oddly intimate move, though he was only touching my shoe.

"I'll figure it out," he said.

"I believe you," I said. "And if you don't, you'll have a lot of interesting stories going."

And that's when I figured out what Benjamin did. With a clear and classic aha moment.

Aaron dropped off our food.

"Can I get you anything else?" he asked.

"Everything looks great," I said.

We should have set some kind of prize for the one who figured out the other person's secret first.

But, I decided as I dipped a cheese stick into marinara, I

wasn't going to tell him just yet. I was going to wait for the right time.

And give him a little more time figure me out.

He was close, I'd give him that. And as inventive as he was, it wouldn't take him long to figure it out.

Unfortunately, if he didn't figure it out soon, our evening would be over we would go back to just being two strangers who had met on a plane.

14

BENJAMIN

*A*s I munched on my French fries, I watched Brooklyn. I was close to being right. So close I could feel it.

I'd added in too much detail, though. Too much detail had been easy for her to deny. But somewhere in there I had touched on a kernel of truth.

I was almost certain about the independently wealthy part. She hadn't confirmed or denied that part. Another sign that I was on the right track.

She had the look of wealth. She wore designer shoes with red bottoms. And even though I had overlooked it before, I saw that she carried a designer handbag.

Her brunette hair had those subtle highlights that a girl could only get by sitting hours in a salon chair. Highlights were pricy if done right and hers were done right.

It wasn't just her hair and clothes, it was in the way she spoke. In the way she carried herself.

She had been raised with what my grandmother would call good breeding. I would call it polite and refined. She was cultured.

So I had a basic sketch of how she came to be on my

airplane. I maintained that she was independently wealthy. Just not a widow. That came as a relief.

I liked her, but if she had a child… I didn't know. That could change things.

"You look like you're deep in thought," she said, starting on her salad.

"Sorry," I said. "I do that sometimes."

"Occupational hazard?" she asked.

"Tricky," I said. "You're tricky."

She smiled. "Not really."

Brooklyn, I had noticed, had many different smiles. She had a professional smile which was kind and caring. She had a playful smile which was innocent and fun. And she had a secret smile, one that spoke of mystery with a bit of sexiness.

Having discovered this in the short time I had known her, I found myself curious about what other kinds of smiles she might have. Did she have a sexy smile? A surprised smile?

"Do you have pictures?" she asked.

"Pictures of what?" I had the crazy thought that she was asking if I had pictures of her different smiles.

"Your nieces," she said, like maybe I was an idiot.

"Of course."

"Can I see them?"

Pulling out my phone, I pulled up a picture of the twins and laid it in on the table in front of her.

"Cute," she said.

"There are others," I said, reaching over and sliding back to one of my sister holding the two babies.

"Your sister looks tired."

"I'm sure." I glanced away, taking a sip of water.

Now she was looking at a picture of me holding one of the babies. She had a curious expression on her face.

"You look natural with them." When she looked up, her brow was knitted. "Do you have children of your own?

I shook my head quickly. "No children."

And there was a new smile I hadn't seen before. I wasn't quite sure what this one meant.

She slid my phone back.

"What are their names?"

"The babies?" Uh oh. This could be really hard to explain.

She nodded.

"Savannah and Brooklyn." I said it fast, thinking maybe she wouldn't really hear me. Maybe she just asking to be nice and didn't really want to know.

But I was not so fortunate. She leaned forward.

"I'm sorry," she said. "I couldn't really hear you."

I sighed. I could lie about it. I could make something up. But I just didn't want to. I rarely had reason to lie and I didn't want to start with Brooklyn.

"Savannah and Brooklyn," I said.

She looked at me with an expression I couldn't define. Blank. That was the best I could come up with to describe this particular expression.

15

BROOKLYN

$\mathcal{I}$t seemed quiet without the bridal party. It wasn't quiet. It just seemed quiet.

The guys were still yelling at the television and the music still spilled from the speakers.

Benjamin's sister had named her twins Savannah and Brooklyn. Brooklyn.

"That's an odd coincidence, isn't it?" I said.

"A little," he said with a tight smile.

I studied him as the server came and took away our plates and wiped down our table.

As flight attendants, we didn't wear name tags. There was no way he could have known my name. I rarely gave passengers my name unless there was a need. I hadn't had a need to tell anyone on the flight where I had met Benjamin.

I tried to remember. Had I even told him my name? Then I remembered that Grandpa had briefly introduced us.

But that had to be *after* his sister had named her children.

I shook it off. It was just one of those odd coincidences.

"So… what happens if I figure out what you're working on before you figure out why I was on your airplane?"

"I guess you win."

"We didn't talk about prizes."

"We can talk about them now."

I smiled. Benjamin was quick on his feet.

"Okay."

"If I win," he said. "You have to take me to dinner."

"We just had dinner."

"A different dinner," he said with a look.

"And if I win?"

"Then I have to take you to dinner."

"This game seems rigged."

He laughed. "It's your game."

"Your prizes."

"Touché."

The music changed to a softer song I could barely hear and the couple next to us got up and left.

"So you've figured out my project?" he asked.

"Yes," I said. "I'm just trying to decide whether or not I want to tell you."

"You want me to go first."

I gave him a face. "We have to discuss the terms of your surrender."

"I didn't say I was giving up," he said.

"You got anything that doesn't involve me being a widow?"

He hesitated. "I think you're independently wealthy."

I crossed my arms on the table and leaned forward. "You're not entirely correct and you're not entirely wrong."

"Are you going to tell me?"

"Not yet."

"I didn't think so."

"I don't want to spoil all your fun at figuring me out."

"Fair enough. Your turn then."

"You're a writer."

The surprised look on his face was enough to tell me that I was right.

16

BENJAMIN

"How did you figure that out?" I asked.

"It wasn't hard. I knew you were writing something. And then I noticed that you are far too creative at coming up with stories about who I am."

"I gave myself away." Not that I really minded her knowing. "I guess I owe you dinner."

"I guess you do."

"How would I get in touch with you to set this up?"

She held out her hand, palm up.

I put my hand over hers.

"Your phone," she said, giving me that look again.

"Right." I released her hand, unlocked my phone, put it in her palm.

She keyed in something, then pressed a button, and handed it back.

"You can text me," she said.

"No phone calls?"

"I'm a generation Z. It's what we do."

"I'm an old-fashioned Millennial," I said. "But I can adapt." Thankfully, being a young Millennial.

She smiled. "Good to know."

The server came back again. A different server. This fellow was a few years older than Aaron.

"Aaron went on break," he said. "Can I get you anything Miss Johnson? A desert perhaps?"

"Not for me." She glanced in my direction.

"I'm good," I said.

"Let me know if you change your mind," he said.

"I will. Thank you."

Everyone, it seems, knew Brooklyn by name.

And now, I knew her last name.

Brooklyn Johnson. Mystery girl.

Everyone seemed to know her except me.

But this wasn't my usual scene. I mostly stayed to myself. I went from my condo to the airport, then home again.

I liked it that way.

Brooklyn, however, seemed to be a social butterfly.

She and I were opposites.

And yet I was drawn to her like a moth to a flame.

She checked her phone.

"I have to go," she said, her brow furrowed.

"Is everything okay?"

She glanced up at me distractedly. "Of course. Everything is fine. I just forgot I was supposed to be somewhere."

It felt a little like being punched in the gut. She probably had a date.

"I'll get the ticket."

"No need," she said, with a wave of her hand. "It goes on the company account."

The company account.

The more time I spent with Brooklyn, the less I seemed to know about her.

And the more I wanted to know.

17

BROOKLYN

I had completely forgotten that I was supposed to meet Richard tonight.

Peter punched in the code, drove through the gate, and parked the car in front of Richard's condo off of York Street.

Richard and I had been friends since college. We'd connected at first simply because we were both Houstonians.

He was married now and had two children.

Peter opened the door and I hurried up to Richard's door. He opened it before I could knock.

"I am so sorry," I said. "Time got away from me."

Richard's condo was always immaculate. He collected art, mostly impressionistic, giving his place a very refined appearance.

"Wine?" he asked.

"No. Thanks. I'm good." I sat at his kitchen table.

"At least tell me you were on a date."

I looked up at him and as he set a cold water bottle on the table in front of me. "You were on a date."

"Not really," I said.

"Not really is better than no."

I smiled. Being happily married, Richard insisted that I, too, needed to be happily married or at least in a relationship.

"Just drinks with a Skye Travels customer," I said. "There was a mix up."

"Sometimes mix ups can lead to good things," he said.

"You're right," I said. "That's how we become friends, isn't it?"

"See. Good things." He smiled smugly. "How was Boston?"

"You know." I twisted the top off the water bottle. "I didn't even get out."

"You, my dear, are slipping."

"I am not."

"When is the last time you went out?"

"I went out tonight," I said. "Sort of." I added at his look.

"It's okay," he said. "I'm leaving you alone for now. But only because I have something to show you."

He opened his iPad and pulled up a spreadsheet.

"You've been busy," I said.

"You know I don't play."

"Why do you think I picked you to go into business with?"

"For my good looks," he said.

I laughed. "Right. If only you weren't taken."

"You had your chance."

I knew he wasn't kidding about that. Richard and I were good friends—really good friends, but I knew he'd always liked me.

We got down to business.

Richard was good.

He and I had been top of our class.

I was really surprised it took us this long to figure out how we could go into business together.

As we worked, I couldn't stop thinking about Benjamin.

I'd given him a ride back to the terminal for his car and

before he opened his door, he'd leaned over and kissed me on the cheek.

"I'll see you soon," he'd said.

From the way I couldn't stop thinking about him, soon couldn't get here fast enough.

I forced myself to stop thinking about him so I could concentrate on what Richard was telling me.

That lasted about two seconds.

18

BENJAMIN

I was a man of routine. I'd found that the more things I did on autopilot, the more I freed up my brain for work.

So today, like every day, my alarm went off at four a.m. sharp. And like always, I got out of bed and made my way to the kitchen.

Freshly brewed coffee waited for me. I put a splash of milk and a dab of caramel in my frother, then, after heating all up, added it to my coffee.

I took my cup of coffee outside to my twenty-sixth-floor balcony, sat in my lounge chair, and watched the sunrise. This was my favorite time of day.

I liked watching the world wake up.

Before the sun even came over the horizon, the sky turned orange. An orange ombre. Lighter at the top and darker toward the horizon. Sunlight reflected off the cluster of downtown skyscrapers as the sun peeked over the horizon.

I'd lived here for almost four years and I never got tired of my view. In the evenings, I could go around to the balcony on the western side of my condo and watch the sunset, but in summer, I didn't go outside in the evenings. I preferred to stay out of the scorching sun. But then, I'd recently starting spending most of summers at my mountain cabin.

I wondered what Brooklyn was doing. Was she an early riser or did she stay up late and sleep late?

As a stewardess—I just liked that word better than flight attendant—she probably had an erratic schedule.

Maybe one day I would find out.

I used my phone to take a photo of the sunrise and thought about texting it to Brooklyn. But it didn't seem like I knew her well enough to text her this early in the morning. Or to text her a picture taken from my balcony. She didn't know where I lived so it might come as a shock to her. I had to err on the side of caution.

I could be wrong about her being independently wealthy. Maybe she had a relative with lots of money. One who could put her on private jets and buy her expensive clothes.

Or maybe she had a man who took care of her. As soon as I had the thought, I dismissed it. The Brooklyn, as I imagined her to be anyway, was innocent and sweet.

Maybe she knew someone at Skye Travels—a stewardess would make contacts, especially with her easy personality—and they gave her a discount. That, I decided, was the solution I liked best.

That would fit with what I knew about her.

Everyone she encountered liked her. It would come as no surprise that she would make friends who would want to help her out.

I went back inside for my second cup of coffee as I considered. If that was the case, they might not charge her anything.

As I heated milk in my frother, I knew I had stumbled upon what had to be the right answer.

Today I would text her. Set up the dinner I owed her.

But first I needed to get some work done.

Going into my home office, I turned on the gas to the fireplace. A comfortable armchair with an ottoman, an end table next to it, was the perfect place to sit and read.

Bookcases covering one wall was filled with books, mostly paperbacks. Although some were double stacked, they were orderly enough that I could put my hand on just about any book I wanted.

I went to my desk overlooking west Houston, opened my computer, and settled in.

As I typed, I added a new character. A young lady with long wavy brunette hair, and sultry eyes. Since I wasn't very far along in the book, my character whom I named Bree, quickly became the love interest of my main character.

The chapter flowed easily. I sat back and let my mind wander. It wove its way around what had already become a familiar path—straight to thoughts of Brooklyn and her jade green eyes.

I was a man besotted.

19

BROOKLYN

*T*he next morning at eight o'clock, I dragged out of bed and padded to the kitchen.

Then I remembered. My cappuccino machine was out of order and I'd forgotten to call in for a repair. So I turned on the electric tea kettle and heated water for instant coffee. It would do. Sometimes I didn't even drink coffee, but today was a little bit cooler, so it seemed like a good idea.

While I waited, I checked my messages.

I had a message from work with a revised schedule. Tomorrow I was scheduled for a flight out to Atlanta and back. Not bad. And not an overnight.

I didn't usually mind overnights, but I was glad to not have one coming up. I had some things to do. My little company was actually taking form. I could even see it now, coming to life. We were getting so close to making it a reality. But I had some paperwork to do.

As I stirred my instant coffee, adding in a heap of sweetener, I wondered if this was how my grandfather had felt when he had started Skye Travels.

He had done the whole thing by himself, at least at first.

Then Grandma had jumped in and helped him. But it had been just him at the very beginning. At least I had Richard along with me.

I sat down at my kitchen table and considered. I had so many family members who would have happily helped me with it. Some might even be hurt that I hadn't asked for their help. We were, after all, a family of entrepreneurs. And we all jumped in to help each other at any opportunity.

But I wanted something that was just mine. Richard didn't count because he wasn't family. Not that I would ever tell him that.

I scrolled through my recent messages. I should have one from last night from an unfamiliar number. I'd sent it myself.

It should simply say *Hello. This is Brooklyn.*

But there was no message like that on my phone. Perplexed, I turned off my phone and restarted it.

I tapped my fingers on the table while I waited for it to power back on.

The message I'd sent from Benjamin's phone was not there.

What had I done?

Surely I hadn't keyed in the wrong phone number. It was true that I never called myself, but still. I should have let him type his number in my phone.

We should have done a crosscheck. I knew to always do a crosscheck. I'd messed up.

That was the only answer. I had given him the wrong number.

Well. This was unfortunate.

The only way I could get in touch with him would be to get his phone number from the Skye Travels records.

Taking a guy's phone number for personal reasons was a lot different from taking a peek at his favorite drink.

I would just wait. Maybe the message just hadn't gone through. I would be patient.

Give things time to happen.

I was meeting my Grandma Savannah for lunch today. I'd ask her what I should do. She would know.

Feeling better, knowing that I had someone I could ask, I went to get a shower.

Just because I wanted to do some things on my own didn't mean I didn't rely on family support when I needed it.

I let the warm water run over my head, washing away the stress.

In some ways, I was a very complicated woman. In other ways I was quite simple. I just wanted the same thing everyone wanted out of life. I wanted to be happy and to have someone to share it with. That did not seem like too much to ask.

20

BENJAMIN

Hello. This is Brooklyn.

I stared at the text Brooklyn had typed into my phone and attempted to send to what I assumed was her phone number.

Message failed.

I powered my phone off and turned it back on. That was the first thing tech support recommended. I know. I'd done it often enough.

I gave it time to populate. For the WIFI to reconnect.

I paced from one side of my condo to the other. West to East and back again. My condo had one of the best views and most of the time it made me happy to live here.

But today not much of anything was making me happy.

When nothing changed, I typed a new message.

Hello. This is Benjamin.

Hit send.

Message failed.

What the—?

I stopped and looked out toward the Galleria. Traffic was backed up today. Not surprising.

I was feeling sick to my stomach.

Surely Brooklyn hadn't given me a wrong number… on purpose.

Would she?

Of course she wouldn't. It would have been an accident.

But… no matter how it happened, the result was the same. I had no way of getting in touch with her.

This was not how I had planned on my day going.

I'd planned to text Brooklyn and set up a date with her, preferably tonight.

I sat down in the armchair in my office and stared into the flames.

I knew where she worked. Sort of. I knew which airline, but it with hundreds… thousands?… of flights going out every day, it would be impossible for me to find her. And airlines didn't give up information like flight attendant schedules, rightly so. It would be concerning if they did.

The flames in my gas fireplace were real, but not the logs or the embers. My fireplace at my mountain cabin used real wood. Wood I chopped with my own hands.

It was rather funny in a sad way that I had enjoyed my little cabin, sitting in front of my real wood burning fireplace, spending hours at the keyboard, sometimes walking into town and wandering the streets of the little town of Whiskey Springs.

Somewhere between the time I had met Brooklyn and now, I had started to include Brooklyn when I pictured myself at my cabin.

And now… all my fantasies about having her in my life

were dissolving like invisible ink on a page. It was as though yesterday had never happened.

I'd spent all that energy trying to figure her out and now I didn't even know how to find her. I hadn't given her my phone number. We had made the cardinal mistake of not crosschecking each other.

I had to believe that it had been a mistake.

The mysteries and problems in my books always worked themselves out.

Unfortunately, I didn't have a solution to this problem.

And this was one that actually mattered to my heart.

21

BROOKLYN

I met Grandma Savannah at one of her favorite French lunch places, Etoile, in Uptown Park, not far from my patio home.

Grandma Savannah was beautiful. She kept herself looking lovely. She ran three miles every day. Had her hair trimmed and styled at least once a month. If she hadn't just come from the salon today, she certainly looked like it. Her shoulder length hair was bouncy and smooth, light brunette, not a single gray hair. Her makeup was tasteful with muted red lipstick.

Like always when she went out in public, she was wearing a pencil skirt with a little suit jacket. Today's suit was a lovely powder blue.

I sincerely hoped that when I grew up I would be like Grandma Savannah.

The restaurant had plenty of patrons, but it wasn't crowded. Music played softly in the background blending easily with pleasant conversations.

We sat at a table by the window and ordered mimosas and salmon benedict.

Even before our drink came, Grandma leaned forward and put a hand on mine.

"How are you, Dear?" she asked.

Grandma was perceptive, one of the most perceptive people I knew. I'd taken time with my own appearance. I, too, had on red lipstick and a white sheath dress with a little matching jacket.

The only way Grandma could possibly know something was wrong had to be in my eyes.

"I'm good," I said, not wanting to start off our conversation with my problems. "You look lovely."

"Thank you," she said as the server dropped off our mimosas. "Your grandfather says hi."

"I saw him yesterday," I said. "He looked good." Was it really just yesterday? It seemed like days ago since I'd flown in from Boston. Part of it, I knew, was that I hadn't seen Benjamin since last night. When I'd dropped him off at the private airport terminal last night, I'd expected to see him soon. Now I didn't know when I would see him again.

And my heart felt bruised because of it.

Maybe Grandma could see my bruised heart. As a gifted psychologist, she worked with people every day who had bruised hearts. She probably had a sense about it.

Settling into her chair, she took a sip of her drink.

"Grandpa said you flew back from Boston with a friend of yours."

Ah. So that's what she was going on. Grandpa had told her something about Benjamin. He had seen how surprised we were to see each other and he'd seen us leave the airport together.

He was an observant man. With the two of them together, a girl didn't stand a chance. I often wondered what it was like for my mother and her three sisters growing up with Grandpa and Grandma as parents. Nothing got past either one of them.

"It's kind of a funny story," I said, swirling my drink before I took a sip.

This was good. I didn't have to figure out how to bring up my problem with finding Benjamin.

Grandma smiled. "You know I like a good story."

Yes, I did know it. She especially liked a good story when it involved the lives of one of her grandchildren.

I told her how I'd met Benjamin on my flight to Boston, leaving out how I'd looked up his drink of choice on the Skye Travels website.

Told her about how Grandpa had let me share his private flight to Houston.

"He told me about that," she said. "He comped his next flight."

"He comped it?" I asked, surprised. That went against good business tactics. I'd expect him to discount it, maybe even half price, but I hadn't expected him to comp it. Surely being in my company wasn't that unpleasant.

Grandma shrugged. "He's getting soft in his old age. Besides Benjamin is a good customer. He's a writer, you know."

"Yes, he told me."

And then it hit me. I'd always thought of writers as starving artists. But Benjamin flew private. Not exactly a starving artist.

All these thoughts, scrambling together in my head had me feeling off-balance.

"Are you going to see him again?" Grandma asked, cutting right to the chase.

I blew out a breath and gave her a little smile.

22

BENJAMIN

Two weeks later

It was a lovely Thursday afternoon. October.

In Houston, October could be hot as hell or it could be pleasantly brisk.

Today was pleasantly brisk.

I'd put my head down and as a result, I was caught up on my writing. First three chapters written and revised four times. Then polished. Deciding it was ready to be sent out in the world, I'd emailed the first three chapters and an outline to my editor. So now it was time to take a break.

I stepped onto the elevator from my living room—a novelty I never tired of—and rode down to the bottom floor.

This was the first time I had been outside the building for two weeks.

Some people would say there was something wrong with me. But those some people were not writers. To me, the perfect day was spent at my computer, typing away, not having anyplace I had to go.

I walked down to Uptown Park and wandered around, not going inside any of the shops. Just wandering, but staying in my own head.

I stopped and sat on a bench beneath an oak tree and just idly watched people, mostly couples.

I was feeling antsy. That was the best way I could describe it.

It had been two weeks since I had discovered that I didn't know how to get in touch with Brooklyn. I checked my messages several times a day. Got nothing other than *Message failed.*

My phone was working. I got messages from my sister. She delighted in sending me pictures of the twins. Instead of using their names when she sent me pictures, she identified one of them as *yours* and the other as *mine.*

There was something wrong with my sister's head.

The cool weather made me want to get out of here. To go to my cabin in the mountains. Maybe I could even catch the first snowfall if I was lucky.

I messaged Noah Worthington to see what the next available flight was. Somehow Noah had become my point of contact. I think it had happened when he gave me his personal number and invited me to call him anytime I needed anything.

While I waited for his answer and watched people, it took me a few minutes before I realized I was looking for a pretty brunette with green eyes. Her image was burned into my mind and I knew that I would know her if I saw her.

But Houston was a big place. A really big place. The odds of me running into her on the street were just about next to impossible.

But I also knew that I would never give up on looking for her.

I heard back from Noah after about thirty minutes.

NOAH

You can fly tomorrow if you don't mind a late flight.

Sounds good. I don't mind.

I'll have the office call to schedule you.

A sense of relief settled over me. At least in the mountains, I wouldn't find myself looking for Brooklyn.

How was a man supposed to find one girl in a world this big?

She was somehow connected to Skye travels. I'd bet on that.

As I walked back to my condo and stepped onto the elevator, it occurred to me that the whole reason I wanted to go to the cabin was so that I could fly with Skye Travels. And maybe, just maybe, I would see Brooklyn.

As unlikely as it was, it was about as close to possible as I was going to get.

23

BROOKLYN

*T*wo weeks had passed since I'd seen Benjamin. I'd made a dozen flights and I'd looked for him on every one of them. Every single one. I did it even though I knew he wouldn't be there.

I took my grandmother's advice and I didn't look him up.

She told me that fate would sort it all out.

She claimed that when the time was right, I'd see Benjamin again. She didn't say *if*. She said *when*. I appreciated her confidence, but I was having trouble sharing it.

I'd made it a point to tell her that he was a regular Skye Travels customer.

She had shaken her head. "That's not the way to go about it," she said.

I fastened my seat belt and prepared to land.

Back in Houston. I'd been away for two days and was ready to get back to my place. Ready to get back to work on my own project.

I still liked my work as a stewardess, but I was starting to feel like there was something else. I was feeling edgy.

I blamed it all on Benjamin.

He'd turned my life upside down.

No matter which path I tried to send my thoughts, they always ended up squarely on him.

It was getting rather annoying, all in all.

Since I couldn't look for him on the Skye Travels data base, I was pretty sure I would never see him again.

I didn't know him that well. You'd think we had been dating for years, the way I had been moping about.

I adjusted my seatbelt and tried to think about what I was going to do on my two days off.

Richard was out of town, so I couldn't meet with him. We were waiting on paperwork to come back anyway.

On Sunday, my grandparents had their weekly family gathering, but that was three days away. I'd probably be on a flight that day.

I could see if my Aunt Brianna was available to go shopping. That sounded good. Or if not her, maybe my new sister-in-law Chloé would want to go. But she was probably working, too. She was the supervising maintenance engineer for Skye Travels. Even those who joined the family by marriage worked for the family.

I was one of the few who went my own way. My mother had gone her own way as a college professor and my grandmother, of course, as a psychologist. So I was not the only one.

Tree and buildings flashed past as we went in for a landing, wheels landing smoothly on the runway.

I could rearrange my house. That was always an interesting activity. I was overdue. I liked to rearrange at least two or three times a year. When I did, I pruned out things I needed to donate or discard. Gave it a good cleaning.

As we taxied to the gate, I decided I'd go by the Skye Travels office and see if the receptionist wanted some time off the next couple of days. I could do the scheduling. Anything to keep from going stir-crazy.

By the time we got everyone off the plane and gave it a quick clean up, I'd lost any motivation to do anything in my house.

Two hours later, I walked through the airport terminal and took a car around to the private Skye Travels building.

The receptionist wasn't in. I checked my watch. It wasn't that late.

Since I didn't see anyone at all, I walked down through the halls toward Grandpa's office.

About halfway down the hall, I met Grandpa Noah coming my way.

"Hey," I said. "Where is everyone?"

"I don't know," he said.

I turned and walked with him.

"Where are you headed?"

"Your brother was scheduled to take a flight, but Chloé had an emergency doctor's appointment."

"Is she okay?"

"Pregnant."

"Why didn't I know this?" I asked, mostly to myself. So Chloé wouldn't be available this weekend.

He stopped and looked at me.

"What are you doing here?"

"Just got in. Had some time."

"How much time?"

"My next flight is supposed to be scheduled for Sunday."

"I'm headed to Whiskey Springs. They're having some trouble learning our scheduling system. Want to come with and help me teach them?"

"There's nothing hard about the system," I said.

"Not when you know it like you do."

I shrugged. As one of the early adapters, I'd had input on it, so yeah, I knew it inside and out.

"Where are your bags?" He looked down as though he expected me to have my luggage with me.

"In the car."

"Come with me," he said.

"To Whiskey Springs? Now?"

He grinned at me. "I could use your help. Unless you have plans for next couple of days."

Since he was my grandfather, I wasn't offended by his assumption that I didn't have plans for the weekend.

"I have to change," I said.

"No need," he said, walking again. "And no time."

24

BENJAMIN

*N*oah sent a message that he was on his way.

I made myself comfortable in the Phenom, taking a bottle of cold water from the refrigerator.

It was rare to get Noah as a pilot, much less twice in a row. It had been my understanding that he had cut back on his flight time for more family time. I'd also heard that he had opened a terminal in Whiskey Springs and was overseeing that project. Probably why he was heading that way, taking me along with him.

I hoped that I had his energy when I was his age.

I wouldn't mind having his energy and drive now.

Powering on my computer, I pulled up my manuscript and reread what I had so far. With a few hours in the air, I could get at least a couple of chapters done.

Once we landed, I had lots to do. I had to go to the grocery store and buy enough supplies for at least a week. I was pretty sure I had enough firewood, but if I didn't I'd be chopping some wood.

But for now, I had uninterrupted work time.

I swirled around with my back to the front of the airplane

so I could put my feet up on the chair behind me and quickly settled into my work.

This chapter was from Bree's viewpoint. I liked writing about Bree. It allowed me to have an excuse to think about Brooklyn.

In my story, I had her dressed in a low-cut, but tasteful red evening gown. High heels. Her hair pulled up on top of her head and falling messily around her face.

It was a pretty picture and I was quickly lost in that world.

I heard someone coming up the stairs of the airplane, but I didn't look up. It would just be Noah and I needed to finish getting this scene down on paper.

"Benjamin," Noah said. "Are you about ready?"

I dropped my feet to the floor—it was just the respectful thing to do—and finished the sentence I was typing. Just a few more words and I would have the conversation in my head down on paper.

"Just about."

There. Done.

I swirled my chair around and just as I faced the front of the airplane Brooklyn came in through the door.

I blinked.

For just a moment, she was Bree.

Except that instead of a red evening gown, she was wearing a black flight attendant's uniform.

But her hair. Her hair was just about the same as I had just described.

She saw me, then looked accusingly at her grandfather.

"Do you mind company?" Noah asked me.

I grinned and closed the lid on my laptop. "Not at all," I said.

Brooklyn looked like a deer in headlights. Not exactly the way I had imagined she would greet me when we finally saw each other again.

Shaking his head, Noah turned and went into the cockpit.

"Sit wherever you like," he told her, over his shoulder. "You can copilot if you want to."

She didn't answer him.

"I didn't know," she said to me.

I unbuckled my seat belt and walked toward her.

She was here and I would figure everything else out somehow.

25

BROOKLYN

randpa Noah should have told me. That was the only thought I could get past my dazed and confused brain.

It was a good thing he was my grandfather. Otherwise I'd feel like he'd brought me here on false pretenses. I knew he wouldn't do that, though.

But above all that, Benjamin was here. Right here.

Déjà vu.

Of the best kind.

"I didn't know," I said.

I looked back for Grandpa Noah, but he was already in the cockpit.

My feet were frozen to the floor.

Benjamin had stood up and was standing in front of me now.

Handsome. Even more handsome than I remembered. My heart was beating much too fast and my hands were shaking. I ran them along my skirt and tried to force a smile.

"Hi," he said.

"Hi."

He took my hands and squeezed them. Then he pulled me into a hug.

I hugged him back. I was so glad to see him.

He was hugging me like he never wanted to let me go.

"Time to sit down," Grandpa said over the speaker.

Benjamin held onto my hand as he led me to my seat.

When he let go of my hand, I realized the plane was moving and I needed to buckle up.

"The message didn't work." We both said it at the same time.

"Can I see it?" I asked.

"Of course." He unlocked his phone and handed it to me.

I looked at the number put a hand over my face.

"I had a dyslexic moment," I said and typed in my number—right this time. This time I called my phone.

When it rang, I pulled it out of my purse and held it up for him to see his number on the screen.

"Wow," he said, taking his phone back when I held it out to him.

"Do you know how lucky we are?"

I shook my head. Then nodded. "They say lightning never strikes in the same place more than once."

"Third times the charm," he said, holding up his phone. "I won't lose you again."

"You're here," I said, still trying to wrap my head around it.

"Last minute impulse."

"I wasn't supposed to be here." I ran a hand in the general direction of my uniform.

"And here we are."

I smiled then. "Here we are. Just like my grandmother said."

"What's that?"

"Nothing."

I looked toward the cockpit where my grandfather sat, deftly piloting the airplane out to the runway.

"You want to have dinner tonight?" he asked.

"You don't waste any time, do you?" I asked, feeling some of the shock wearing off.

"I've got two weeks to make up for."

"Why are you going to Whiskey Springs?" I asked.

"I have a cabin there."

"A cabin."

"Yes. Sometimes I get stir crazy in the city and need to get out to nature."

I nodded, but I didn't really understand the concept.

Born and bred in Houston, the city was what I knew.

"You didn't grow up in the city."

"Ten acres outside of Savannah."

"Wow. That is different."

He was smiling at me again… in that way that sent the good kind of goosebumps along my skin.

"We are so opposite," I said.

26

BENJAMIN

I knew the moment the airplane left the ground. It rocked just a little with nothing more than that little pocket of air separating the airplane from the ground.

As the airplane took flight, seeming to head straight up into the sky, I held out my hand. Brooklyn put hers in mine without any hesitation.

She was as beautiful as any fairy princess. Even more beautiful than I had been able to capture in my descriptions on paper. Maybe if I was an artist, I could try to paint her, but I doubted any painting, even by an acclaimed artist, could ever do her justice.

Her face was in motion. Her jade green eyes watching me. Those eyes spoke volumes. They asked questions. They showed surprise and confusion. They revealed happiness.

"I still don't know your connection to Skye Travels," I said.

I saw the indecision in her eyes. There was something she didn't seem to want to tell me.

"I'm going to help train the staff at the airport terminal in Whiskey Springs. New software."

"Right," I said. She worked for Skye Travels. With her being a stewardess for the major airline, it hadn't occurred to me that she might work for Skye Travels. Two jobs.

She was working two jobs.

I replayed our conversation over dinner at the Sky House restaurant. She'd said she had never been married. But I couldn't remember her ever saying whether or not she had children. I don't remember her saying one way or the other.

My God.

I sat back in my chair. She didn't have to do this. I could take care of her. She would never have to work another day in her life unless she wanted to.

"You should have told me," I said, although I knew she had no reason to.

"Told you what?"

"That you're working two jobs."

"I'm not—"

She stopped in mid-sentence and looked away. I couldn't tell what she was thinking. What she was feeling.

"It's okay," I said. "I won't say anything else about it."

"I thought you were a starving artist," she said. "I don't recognize your name."

"I write under a pen name. My editor thought my real last name, Gray, wasn't catchy, so she switched it."

"Switched it how?"

"I write under Grayson Benjamin."

She smiled, a slow smile. Then she reached into her bag and pulled out my latest book, *The Edge of Danger*. She turned it over and grinned at my picture on the back.

"You look different," she said.

"Should I take that as a compliment?" I teased.

"Not better or worse, just different. Like your name. Different."

"Now you know everything about me," I said.

"I know that can't possibly be true. I had no idea you were a jet-setting, famous author."

"My name's famous," I said. "No one recognizes me. Not exactly jet-setting, either."

If she knew I'd stayed in my condo for two weeks without leaving, I can only wonder what she might think of me. Certainly not jet-setting. Not even close.

But right now, being here on this plane with her, was nothing short of a miracle. I would have bet everything I owned and then some that I would never see her again and if I did, it certainly wouldn't be on a Skye Travels airplane.

27

BROOKLYN

rayson Benjamin. Famous author. Right here. And I was reading his book and hadn't even known it was his book.

Grandma Savannah had been right.

Things would work out as they were supposed to.

I was quite simply astounded. Not that he was famous. I'd met famous people before. But that he was famous and he was here with me and he wanted to take me to dinner.

And there was the minor detail that I was hopelessly attracted to him. And that he seemed to like me.

It would be okay to tell him that I was Noah Worthington's granddaughter. I was honestly surprised that he hadn't figured it out on his own. Of course, Grandpa and I didn't exactly look alike. If he had met Grandma or even my mother, he would most certainly have figured it out.

As a writer, he would be more observant than most men.

"I'm not supposed to ask what you're working on now, am I?" I asked.

"You can ask."

"I've heard that authors don't like to talk about what they're working on."

He shrugged. "I wouldn't talk about it to readers, but…" he stopped and looked at me sideways. Then looked down at the book I was still holding. "Maybe I shouldn't talk to you about it."

I laughed. "I'm a reader," I said. "But don't hold that against me."

"I'm actually working on the next book in that series."

"Oh. Awesome."

"Are you fangirling me?"

"I guess I am." I couldn't stop grinning.

And it wasn't so much that he was one of my favorite authors and I hadn't even put the two together, but it was something else.

It was finding him again. I'd all but given up on ever seeing him again.

The odds had just seemed too astronomical.

And yet despite those odds, I'd been thinking about him all the time. I hadn't even so much as looked at another guy since that day we'd had turbulence on the plane and he had caught me, maybe even saving my life.

If Grandma Savannah hadn't insisted that I leave it alone, I probably would have looked him up on the Skye Travels database. I'd had to talk myself out of it several times. All I wanted was his phone number which he would have given to me. Meant to give me. It would have been scarily easy to justify.

But I had waited. Fortunately, I didn't have to test just how long I would have waited. Two weeks was way, way longer than I would have thought I could go.

My self-restraint was so much more than I thought.

"Is there anything else I need to know about you?" I asked.

"Girlfriend? Wife?" I turned the book over and read his bio. I'd never really read it before, at least not closely. "It doesn't say."

"That's because I'm supposed to be mysterious," he said.

I laughed. "It's working."

"Is it?" he asked. "because I couldn't really tell."

Since he was still holding my hand, I just looked at him and let the stress of the past two weeks fade away like a wispy cloud.

28

BENJAMIN

I hadn't even so much as opened my computer on the flight, but I didn't so much as care even a little.

Holding Brooklyn's hand all the way to Whiskey Springs had made the flight one of the most pleasant I'd had and I'd flown a lot.

I'd probably never want to fly alone again. She had ruined it for me. Now I was going to want to take her with me wherever I went.

Noah made a smooth landing, as always, and taxied to the little terminal. It was already dark, so we couldn't see the mountains or the trees or anything that was stunningly beautiful about Whiskey Springs. On the bright side, she had distracted me from thinking about the mountains that not even Noah could see in the darkness. Thank God for accurate radar.

"Do you have to work tonight?" I asked.

"No," she said. "it's too late. Everyone's gone."

"That's good."

"What about you? Are you going to work tonight?"

"That actually depends on you."

Even as I said it I knew the answer was unequivocally no.

Even if she didn't go to dinner with me and I went straight to my cabin, I knew I wouldn't work. Probably wouldn't even sleep.

My mind would be racing. No doubt.

Now that I had found her, what was I going to do with her?

I doubted she would marry me without at least a real date or two.

But I needed to do something to take her away from at least one of her jobs.

I needed to find out if she had a child, but it was a sensitive area for some women and since she hadn't volunteered it, I felt like I should tread carefully.

Then again, a lot of what I knew about women I'd learned from my sister. And since she was seriously messed up in the head, I had to be careful relying on anything I learned from her.

"I thought we had a date," she said.

"We do."

There was a car waiting to take all of us into town. As we transitioned from the plane to the car, the cold weather was unexpectedly cold. It was always a bit of a shock to the system to go from the warm, low-elevation climate to the cold, high-elevations.

Apparently Noah and Brooklyn had rooms at the Whiskey Springs Saloon.

"Do you need us to reserve a room for you?" Noah asked, once we were settled in the car. He sat up front while Brooklyn and I sat in the back.

"No," I said. "I'm good. I've got my cabin." The thought of going into my cold cabin in the middle of the night was not the least bit inviting. I made a mental note to invest in one of those Nest thermostats so I could have the cabin warmed up before I got here. Since I usually got here during the day, it had never been much of an issue.

The driver stopped to drop Noah and Brooklyn off at the saloon first. I walked Brooklyn to the door of the saloon as the driver stacked her and Noah's luggage just outside the door.

"Do you need help getting your luggage upstairs?" I asked.

"No," she said. "the driver will do that."

"Okay. Sure."

"It's late," she said. "Why don't you just stay here. We can have dinner, then the driver can take you to your cabin."

I glanced at Noah. He was heading inside to do the check-in.

"Sure," I said. "I can do that."

Her smile was worth any discomfort I might have at the thought of possibly having to share my date with Noah Worthington.

It didn't matter, I reminded myself.

I wasn't going anywhere.

Now that I'd found her, there was no way that I was going to let her slip away again.

"Why are you smiling?" she asked.

"I'm not smiling."

She looked at me sideways. "I think you are."

"I'm just happy to be here," I said.

She was looking at me funny. I would have looked at me funny, too.

I blamed my sister. She had inadvertently taught me to act goofy. It couldn't possibly be all that time I spent alone in my head making up my own people.

It couldn't possibly be that.

As long as Brooklyn didn't mind, everything was good.

29

BROOKLYN

*N*oah had reserved us rooms at the Whiskey Springs Saloon. It was, I soon learned, the oldest building in town. It had started out as an actual saloon with rooms on the second floor, some people even living in them while they built their permanent houses or until they moved on to the next place.

The rooms had been updated with electricity and plumbing, but they had mostly maintained their historicalness over the years.

Grandpa went up to his room, but I stayed downstairs with Benjamin.

I loved my Grandpa dearly, but I didn't really want to share my date with him.

I didn't know what Grandpa's plans were. He'd probably stay in his room. Work some and talk to Grandma. Even after all these years, they were still like teenagers in love.

Benjamin and I found an empty table on the side of the saloon away from the piano, enthusiastically played by a young lady wearing a long, ruffled red saloon girl dress. I was a little surprised to hear such talent out here on the edge of nowhere.

It wasn't nowhere, of course. It was a suburb of Denver and, thanks to Grandpa, even had an airport with a terminal and a runway that could handle just about any private jet.

"Martini?" Benjamin asked as a server headed in our direction.

"Sure," I said with a smile.

He ordered two dirty martinis and we took the menus offered by the server.

As we looked over the menus, Benjamin looked over his menu at me.

"What is it?" I asked.

"I don't think this one should count."

"This one what?"

"This dinner. I don't think it should count as our date," he said.

"Why not?" I asked, but I didn't disagree.

"Because you're here for work."

I nodded slowly. "Good point. But… are you sure you're not just trying to get a second date with me?"

"Would that be such a bad thing?"

"Probably not." I shrugged and returned my attention back to my menu.

He watched me for a minute, then smiled to himself and set his menu aside.

"You've already decided what you want?" I asked.

"I like to keep things simple."

"Burger and fries?"

He grinned. "I'm predictable."

"A little." I closed my menu and set it aside with his. "I think I'll have the fish sandwich and fries."

"Sounds good," he said, picking his menu back up. "I think I'll have that, too."

I smiled. I'd think about that feeling of warmth that ran through me later.

"How's your sister? Still trying to pawn one of her babies off on you?"

"She's awful," he said. "Instead of calling them by their names, she refers to them as *yours* and *mine*."

"Which one is yours?" I asked, trying not to laugh.

"I don't know." He had a funny look on his face. "Brooklyn."

"How did that happen?"

"I can't really tell you."

Before I could question him on what he meant by that, the server came to take our order.

30

BENJAMIN

*A*fter the server took our order, I had quickly changed the subject.

I didn't want to tell her how my sister's baby named Brooklyn came to be thought of as *mine* by her. I didn't want to lie, but I didn't want to tell this Brooklyn that I had suggested the name because I'd been thinking about her.

As we ate, the atmosphere seemed to change over to a slightly more rowdy nighttime crowd. More people at the bar and fewer people at the tables.

I didn't usually come into town at night. I'd done my share of partying in college and was settled now. My sister seemed to think I was going to make someone a good husband and I was inclined to believe her. I just hadn't been so inclined as to actively seek out who exactly that wife might be. Until now. And then the right one just kind of fell into my lap.

The fish sandwich had been a good choice. As we finished eating, I began thinking ahead. Thinking about seeing her again. We didn't have anything definite set up.

"How long will it take you to train them on the software?" I asked.

"I don't know. I have to fly back Saturday afternoon, so I guess I have a day. Maybe a day and a half at most."

"Too bad," I said. "We could hike up to the falls."

"That sounds nice."

"Maybe you'll finish early and we can go Saturday morning."

"Maybe," she said, distractedly. "We'll see how it goes." She pulled out her phone.

"Everything okay?"

"I think so," she said with a quick glance in my direction. "But… Gr—Noah has to fly back to Houston."

"Tonight?"

"I'm not sure." She glanced at her watch. "I'm going up to see if I can find out."

"Do you need me to stay? To wait for you?"

"No," she said. "I need to pay."

"Don't worry about that," I said. "I'll take of it."

The group of men shouting at the television were louder now. Rowdy.

"I'll walk you upstairs," I said. "Then I'll be at my cabin. Just call if you need me."

"I will," she said.

Heads turned in her direction as we walked across the restaurant, pass the bar, and up the stairs. She didn't even realize it. I don't think she even had a clue just how attractive she was.

"This is his room," she said, knocking. "We'll talk tomorrow."

"Sure," I said. Then I stood there with my hands in my pockets as Noah let her in and they closed the door behind them.

Nope. I was not counting this as a date.

Granted, it had been a while since I had been on a date, but

I was pretty sure, a date still included a goodnight kiss. Or at least the option for one.

And tonight didn't fit that paradigm. Not even a little.

I glanced at my watch. While I had a car and driver at my disposal, I would make a quick stop to get some supplies, then head off to my cabin.

Brooklyn would be okay. She was with her boss. Noah Worthington was old enough to be her grandfather.

Besides, she could take care of herself.

It was a testament to just how besotted I was with her that I didn't want to leave her here alone at the rowdy saloon.

31

BROOKLYN

*T*he next day passed quickly and the two ladies I was charged with training caught on faster than I had been led to believe they would. They were both fast learners. What they did know, they had figured out to do on their own.

Overall, I was quite impressed with them.

We sat in one of the offices at the Whiskey Springs airport terminal. This office had just a small, high rectangular window, obviously not designed for spending any quality time in. I couldn't help but think that it had probably been designed as more of a storage room or maybe a break room. I would hate to have to spend my days locked away in here in a room without a view, especially since the view was so gorgeous.

I had to think they hadn't sorted all the space out yet. The terminal had only been completed for a few months.

Whiskey Springs was high in elevation, surrounded by tall rugged snow-capped mountains with clusters of white clouds around them.

If I had to guess, I'd say it was snowing up there on the mountain peaks. According to the two ladies, one late middle-aged and one early thirties, the first snowfall of the season was expected any day. They were surprisingly looking forward to it.

They said most everyone looked forward to the first snowfall. Of course the downside was that the snow, even though beautiful, could be lethal if not treated with caution and respect. So a lot of people had mixed feelings about the snow that came after the first one, if nothing else.

Grandpa had flown out that morning to take care of something in Houston. I felt a little bit stranded without an airplane here. Or a car. Both ladies had a car and both of them had assured Grandpa that one of them would drive me back into town.

Tomorrow, Grandpa would send someone, even if it wasn't him, back with an airplane to pick me up.

If something came up, all I had to do was to call and someone would be here. Normally, Skye Travels had an airplane housed here, but at the moment, it was sitting in Florida waiting to pick up a passenger.

I had my computer screen projected on the wall as I went through all the scheduling permutations. It really wasn't all that much to learn after they got the basics down. And since they had hands on experience, they caught on quickly.

I sat back and clasped my hands in front of me.

"Questions?" I asked.

"I don't. Not right now," the older lady named Betty said. "This has been very helpful. I don't think we'll have any problems taking it from here.

When the front door opened, we all looked at each other. No one was scheduled to be here today. No flights coming in and none going out. Incoming flights were always subject to change, of course.

"I'll go check," Betty said.

"Should we go with her?" I asked Caroline, the younger girl, as I powered off the computer.

"No," Caroline said. "She'll be fine." She gathered up their legal pad and pens.

I wasn't used to such an isolated environment. Back at Skye Travels in Houston, there were always people around. Anyone working in the office was rarely left alone and if they were, the external doors would be locked.

As I was stashing my laptop in my leather computer bag, Betty came back to the door.

"There's someone here to see you," she said. She looked a little flushed, like she had been jogging.

"Go ahead," I told Caroline. "I've got this."

"No," Betty. "Someone to see you, Brooklyn."

"Me?" Who could be here to see me? I didn't know anyone in Whiskey—

Betty stepped aside and I saw Benjamin standing behind her.

Now I saw why Betty looked a bit breathless. She couldn't possibly be immune to Benjamin's good looks.

He was wearing a black leather jacket, a white shirt, and jeans. His shades tucked in his collar, he looked slightly windblown.

Then I forgot that there was anyone else in the room.

He smiled at me as he brought a bouquet of colorful wildflowers from behind his back and held them out to me.

My heart swooned. Yes, it actually swooned.

"I think we have a date," he said, with a smile that would melt any girl's heart.

"Do we?" I couldn't get my brain to work. I'd just seen him last night, but seeing him here now was somehow more surreal. The other two times I'd seen him had started by coincidence, but tonight he was here intentionally. He had purposely sought me out.

I'd thought about him all day. Wondered if I would see him again before I had to go back to Houston tomorrow.

We had left things so unfinished.

"I hope we do," he said. "Brooklyn. Can I take you to dinner?"

Somewhere in the corner of my eyes, I saw Betty with her hands clasped together beneath her chin and Caroline grinning like a loon.

You'd think he was proposing marriage from their reactions.

"Yes," I said, realizing that a marriage proposal was something I wouldn't mind. Not from Benjamin.

I was in over my head with this one.

And I was going down with the ship.

32

BENJAMIN

*A*fter spending the night in my cabin, pacing around, waiting for the heat to push away the chill of the cold house, I didn't get any writing done.

But I did come to some major conclusions about my life.

One, I no longer wanted to spend it alone. Somewhere in the last couple of weeks—and yes, I could pinpoint the exact moment—the appeal had faded.

Second. I wanted to share my life with Brooklyn.

Third, in order make the first two things happen, I was going to have to put forth the necessary effort.

What that necessary effort was took a bit more strategy.

But being the chess player that I was and the writer that I was, I was able to cobble together those two skills into some semblance of a plan.

I also called my sister.

She might be messed up in the head, but she was not only a female, she was married with children. And she knew better than anyone else.

I'd taken what she suggested and rolled it into a strategy all my own that fit my particular situation.

Since calling or texting Brooklyn seemed impersonal and awkward, I decided to just show up since I knew where she was today. This particular move would have been far more difficult to carry out in Houston and I only had one night here to make it happen, so I had to move fast. My window was fleeting.

Seeing her again, unexpectedly like this, almost backfired on me. I'd intended to surprise her and sweep her off her feet, but she floored me with just how beautiful she was.

And she was just standing there with a power cord in her hands. She, too, was wearing jeans, but she was wearing a suit jacket. Her hair fell loose over her shoulders.

It was her eyes that nearly knocked me down. Those beautiful jade green eyes that looked at me like I was the only man she had ever looked at like this.

And from this point on, I hoped that maybe I would be.

"Excuse me, ladies," I said. "Our car is waiting."

After picking up Brooklyn's computer bag, I took her hand and led her out of the building.

The cold wind splashed against our skin and tousled our hair as I held the door open for her. I hadn't hired a driver. I wanted to drive just so I could be alone with her.

"Where would you like to go?" I asked.

"I don't know." She held the flowers close to her.

"Good," I said, with a smile. "We'll go with my plan."

"You have a plan?"

"Of course," I said. "I'm a chess player, remember?"

"Where are we going?" she asked with a little nod.

"Just Whiskey Springs. The weather looks a bit uncertain right now to go very far."

"Agreed."

She waited a minute. Then. "Are we going back to the saloon?"

"No," I said. "Somewhere better. The Hungry Biscuit."

I tried not to laugh at the expression on her face. Apparently she wasn't familiar with the local establishments and their unique names.

33

BROOKLYN

*T*he fresh wildflowers filled my senses as Benjamin drove down the winding roads.

As the sun dipped below the mountain peaks, it splashed a rainbow of colors across the sky. The misty clouds still hung around the peaks, but the rest of the sky was a beautiful clear blue.

Benjamin had rented a car. It didn't make sense that he rented a car just to drive me from the airport into Whiskey Springs, but he had.

I think it was the bouquet of wildflowers that had charmed me off my feet. He hadn't brought a red rose like most guys would have. He'd brought me a bouquet of flowers that he could have gone out and picked himself right here in the mountains. The two daffodils tucked in among the others flowers with their strong, heady scent were my favorite. The fresh clean scent reminded me of clear summer mornings when I had nothing I had to do except run outside and play with my siblings.

Before we all began the process of adulting.

We pulled into the crowded parking lot of the Hungry

Biscuit. Instead of trying to park like I had expected him to, he valeted the car. The Hungry Biscuit didn't look like the kind of place that valeted and since I didn't see a valet station, I wondered if maybe Benjamin had worked out something ahead of time.

The restaurant was crowded on the inside, too, but we didn't have to wait.

After Benjamin gave his name to the hostess, she led us to a booth in the back with a reserved sign on it. It was the only table that had a candle. Dinner by candlelight.

"Did you make all this happen?" I asked after the hostess left us.

"I might have made some prior arrangements," he said.

A young male server brought two glasses of sparkling water and a bottle of champagne in a silver bucket of ice.

"Champagne?" Benjamin asked.

"Yes please."

The server popped the cork and filled two flutes with the sparkling wine.

"What are we celebrating?" I asked.

"Chance," he said, holding up his flute. "To chance."

I tipped my glass against his, then drank to chance.

What he was calling chance, I was calling destiny.

When everything lined up so perfectly, it couldn't possibly be chance.

"My sister wants to meet you," he said.

"What?" Such a simple statement that sent trepidation through my heart.

"My sister. She wants to meets you. She can't travel right now, but we can fly out to Boston to see her."

"Does she think if there are two of us, we'll take one of her babies?" I was only halfway jesting. A new mother could be desperate.

Benjamin laughed. "Probably. It's like you already know her."

"I have enough cousins and siblings to know how families are."

"What's it like?" he asked. "Being from a big family?"

"I don't know. It's just normal. Except that there are lots of us. And there is always someone there to help out."

He was looking at me funny now.

"Are there a lot of children in your family?"

"More every day."

"What about you?"

I sipped the champagne. "What about me what?"

"Do you hope to have children? One day?"

"Of course," I said, setting my glass aside. "One day." This was a serious conversation. This and he wanted me to meet his sister.

I tried to remind myself that it was only fair since he'd met my grandfather and who knows how many other members of my family as a Skye Travels customer. We were anything but short of pilots in the family.

The thing was. He didn't know they were my family.

He thought I worked there. He thought I had two jobs.

And I'd let him believe it. I had not corrected him.

And now I was starting to feel bad about it.

Deception was not a good way to start off a relationship.

If I'd had any doubt that he wanted a romantic relationship, after tonight those traces of doubt were gone. Vanished.

He couldn't be more clear if he'd come right and asked me to go steady with him.

The thought made me laugh out loud.

I tried to hide the bubble of laughter behind my champagne flute, but nothing got past Benjamin.

"What's funny?" he asked.

"I'm not laughing," I said, trying to straighten my face.

I wasn't laughing because it was funny. I was laughing because I liked him and the thought of going steady with him had my heart fluttering.

I was falling for this guy, hook, line, and sinker.

But I had to be cautious.

34

BENJAMIN

I made a note to myself that Brooklyn had a low tolerance for champagne. She was giggling like a schoolgirl and she wouldn't tell me what was funny.

Maybe I shouldn't have brought up my sister so soon. She probably thought it was funny that I thought she would go with me to Boston so soon.

I didn't seem to be able to help myself. I wanted her near me all the time. I felt like our heartstrings had gotten entwined.

Unfortunately, she didn't seem to feel the same way.

"It's okay," I said, stepping backwards. "I'll tell her the timing isn't good. That you have to work."

"I do have to work."

"I could talk to Noah. Maybe get you a weekend off."

She was already shaking her head. "Please don't do that."

"Okay." I held up a hand. "I won't. I promise."

With such a big family, maybe she was helping to support them. Maybe she worked more than one job because she needed the money to help out her family.

I could respect that.

"You'll let me know if there's something I can do to help?"

"Help with what?"

"Anything."

"Okay."

Leaning across the booth, I put a hand over hers.

"Brooklyn," I said. "I have to be honest with you."

She wasn't laughing any more. Now she was looking confused.

"I'm worried about you working so much."

"I like what I do."

"I know. I understand."

"Benjamin," she said. "It's not so much as it seems. I promise I'm not overworked."

"Okay," I said, sitting back. I'd already pushed too hard.

It was too soon. I was moving too fast and I was going to frighten her away.

"What would you like to eat?" I asked, picking up a menu. "No sandwich and fries tonight."

"Are you trying to impress me?" she asked, with a little smile.

"I don't know. Is it working?"

"Maybe a little."

She smiled at me now.

She was turning me inside out. She had me completely confused.

"Alright," she said, setting her menu aside. "I'll have the lobster."

"Lobster? Good choice."

She had me a little worried when she finished off her glass of champagne.

But, I reminded myself, she wasn't driving.

I really needed to find a way to temper my protectiveness toward her.

Modern women liked to take care of themselves. They didn't like to think that they needed a man to take care of them.

"How long have you worked for Noah?" I asked.

There was that deer in the headlights look again.

She tapped her empty glass and I assumed she was thinking.

"Would you like some more champagne?" I asked, mostly just to give her the chance to think without me just staring at her.

"Yes. Thank you."

I filled her glass with champagne and set the bottle back in the bucket. I'd hardly touched mine. And now I wasn't going to drink more than a few sips.

I had to have a clear head to be responsible for such a beautiful woman.

"Here's the thing," she said, looking up at me from beneath her lashes.

35

BROOKLYN

I was feeling a little bit giddy. It wasn't the champagne. I had mimosas with my grandmother for lunch all the time.

I couldn't quite tell what it was. Not exactly, but I knew it had something to do with Benjamin.

He wanted to know how long I'd worked for Noah Worthington.

This was the tipping point.

I had to tell him now. It was now or never. And if I went with never, I had to never see him again.

Being part of my family meant family gatherings. Family gatherings included boyfriends and girlfriends. So there was no way for me to continue to socialize, much less date him unless I told him. And I had to tell him now.

I took a deep breath and went for it.

"I don't work for Noah," I said.

"Oh," he said, thinking for second. "You're a consultant."

I hadn't thought of that. I almost said yes. But that would put me right back where I was.

I shook my head. "No," I said. "I'm not a consultant."

He was looking at me funny now and turned a little bit green.

"Not that," I said. "Geez. Don't even go there."

"What then?"

I tapped my fingers against the table. Why was this so hard? He knew my family. He shouldn't be shocked.

"Noah is my grandfather." I said it really fast, thinking maybe he wouldn't hear me, I guess.

"Your grandfather?"

"Yes. I know I should have told you."

Benjamin looked at me blankly. Then he was laughing.

"This is perfect." Then he stopped laughing and leaned forward. "Are you serious?" Because you don't look like him."

I rolled my eyes and pulled out my phone. Found a picture of Grandpa Noah and Grandma Savannah.

Held it up for him to see.

"Do I look like her?"

He studied the photo for a moment, then looked at me.

"Somewhat, yes," he said. "Is that Noah's wife?"

"My grandmother."

I swiped and found a picture of my mother. Held it up.

"How about her?"

"Yes. Somewhat."

I had one more card up my sleeve.

I had a picture of me and my Aunt Brianna. Everyone said I looked like her.

"What about her?"

"Are you twins?"

"Be serious."

"I am serious."

"That's my Aunt Brianna."

He was still looking at me like he didn't quite believe me.

"You still don't believe me?"

"I believe you," he said. "I just wish you'd felt comfortable enough to tell me."

"I am telling you," I said. "Aren't you careful who you tell that you're a famous writer?"

He shrugged. "Yes. But no one cares."

"I care." I looked into his deep blue eyes. "So you don't have to worry about me working too much."

"But you work for the big airline."

I sat back. Watched the bubbles in the champagne flute.

"I wanted to be independent. To make my own way."

His lips quirked with a little smile. "You didn't get very far away from airplanes."

I smiled. "No. I didn't. What can I say? It's in my blood."

"I think you and I have a lot in common," he said.

"How so? Do you have jet fuel in your blood, too?"

"No. But instead of becoming the attorney my family expected me to become, I became a writer."

"Did you go to law school?

"Licensed in the state of Texas."

"But you don't use it."

"Only in my fiction."

"Are they upset with you? Your family?"

"Probably. Except my sister. She doesn't care."

"They have to be proud of you, at least now."

"You would think so," I said. "But no matter how many books I write, they don't think I'm doing real work."

"At least I don't have that. As long as we're working, my family is okay with what we do."

"Consider yourself lucky."

"I do." I took another swallow of my champagne. "So now what do we do?"

I smiled a slow smile at me.

"I think I should kiss you."

36

BENJAMIN

*B*rooklyn laughed.

I couldn't tell if it was nervous laughter or happy laughter or confused laughter.

I decided to go with happy laughter. It was the only way to preserve my ego.

"How did you come to that conclusion?" she asked.

"How could I not? I've wanted to do it since the day we met."

She nodded slowly. "Okay."

"Are you coming over here or—"

Before she finished her sentence, I was out of my booth and sliding in next to her.

"Or am I coming over there?" she belatedly finished her sentence.

"I'll come over here," I said.

"You're kind of funny," she said.

I was heartened that she didn't say I was kind of weird.

She was looking up at me with questions. So many questions.

"How do we—"

I leaned down and pressed my lips against hers, answering all her questions at once.

It was supposed to just be a chaste first kiss.

But now that I'd had a taste of her, I wanted more.

So I kissed her again, this time I really kissed her, pulling her close.

She was so… everything. I pulled her into my lap and kissed her until the server came to our booth.

"Um, Sir?"

I set her down and looked at the young boy. His face was red.

"We're not supposed to this in here?"

The boy looked over his shoulder, then leaned forward and whispered. "I don't care. It's my boss."

"Understood," I said, holding up my hands. "It won't happen again."

When the boy didn't leave, I got up and went back to my side of the booth.

"See?" I said. "we're all good."

"Thank you," the boy said.

I glanced over at Brooklyn. Her lips were swollen and slightly parted. I winked at her.

"I think we're ready to order now."

The boy looked dubious. Surely they weren't going to kick us out.

I leaned forward. "I'll double your tip," I said.

"Okay," the server said. "I'll convince my boss that it was a misunderstanding." He glanced at Brooklyn. "Or something."

"Thank you so much," I said.

After he took our orders and walked away, finally, and I looked back over at Brooklyn, she burst into laughter.

"We're so getting kicked out."

"They won't kick us out," I said. *Hopefully.* "You are Noah Worthington's granddaughter and I'm not only a famous writer, I own a home here."

She was looking at me with a little bit of disbelief.

"Okay," I said. "It's only a small cabin, but I pay my taxes."

"I don't know," she said, looking over my shoulder.

The manager, a middle-aged, slightly overweight fellow wearing a tie and a cowboy hat—the two looked very strange together to me—came up to our table.

"Hi," I said.

"Hi. You two just visiting?"

"I have a cabin here," I said.

"And he's a famous writer," Brooklyn said. "Grayson Benjamin."

I groaned. "Please accept my apology. It wasn't Miss Worthington's fault."

The manager looked confused a moment, then looked over at Brooklyn.

"Worthington?"

"Yes," she said, cutting her eyes at me.

"Related to Noah Worthington?"

She nodded, glaring at me now. I just shrugged.

"My apologies ma'am," he said. "It's a pleasure to have you dine with us."

"Thank you for your understanding," she told him, then shifted her gaze back to me. If looks could kill… "We had a bet to settle."

"A bet?" I said after the manager left.

"It was the best I could come with in a moment's notice. Besides, you told him who I was."

I lifted an eyebrow. "Grayson Benjamin. Famous writer?"

"It would have worked."

"I guess we'll never know which one worked."

"Maybe it was the synergy."

"Good word, Miss Worthington."

"You are trouble, Mr. Gray."

37

BROOKLYN

I decided I needed a second glass of champagne after all. I hadn't been planning to drink it, but my thoughts were all jumbled and I was a mess.

Not that the champagne would help with my thoughts, but maybe it would settle my nerves.

Benjamin had nearly gotten us kicked out of the restaurant by kissing me. And not just kissing me, but *kissing* me.

I could not remember ever having been kissed quite so thoroughly and certainly not in public. Such behavior, it seemed, was not appreciated in Whiskey Springs, or at least not in the Hungry Biscuit.

It wasn't like anyone was paying us any attention. But I saw his point. There were a couple of children sitting at a table with their parents.

Our food came shortly. We may not be kicked out, but we were being rushed out.

When I caught Benjamin looking at me, he smiled.

He was having a profound effect on my system. My hand shook as I stabbed the asparagus on my plate.

He so should not have ravished me that way in the restaurant.

But I so wanted him to do it again.

My lips still tingled from his or maybe it was the champagne. Hard to say. Either way, my nerves were definitely still reeling from the unexpected.

I took a bite of lobster and sighed.

I was in trouble.

Now that Benjamin had gone and kissed me, it was all I could think about.

He, however, seemed unaffected. He attacked his food with gusto. As though nothing had happened.

I scowled at him, but he just smiled.

"Want to walk downtown and get some ice cream after this?"

"Okay," I said. It wasn't that I wanted ice cream, it was that he and I needed to leave this restaurant as quickly as possible.

I firmly believed that the only reason we hadn't been kicked out was because Benjamin threw out my last name. And the funny thing was my last name wasn't Worthington. My last name was Johnson. But I didn't try to deny it. I did, after all, have Worthington blood on my mother's side.

After dinner, we walked outside into the cold night air. Benjamin wrapped an arm around me pulling me close against him.

I was pleasantly surprised by his open affection. He did not seem to care who saw us together.

"You should see this place during the summer," he said. "Lots of tourists."

"You're not a tourist." It wasn't really a question. Just an observation.

"I think I am. I live in Houston. This is just my little getaway."

"For writing."

"Mostly," he said.

"You aren't getting much writing done this trip."

"It's okay," he said. "I'm working on a different kind of investment."

A different kind of investment.

As we stepped into Smedley's Ice Cream Shop, I couldn't help but wonder at his odd choice of words. As a writer, he used his words with intention.

Was that how he thought about me? As an investment?

He was a writer. A successful writer.

But… how long had he known who I was?

"What kind of ice cream do you want?" he asked, squeezing me close.

"Just a chocolate vanilla swirl," I said with a tight smile.

What had I done?

I had fallen for a man who saw me as an investment.

At least I found out now.

Before I got in too deep.

38

BENJAMIN

*W*e sat at Smedley's Ice Cream Parlor along with a dozen other people. Popular music played over the speakers in the background.

Brooklyn toyed with a small cup of chocolate vanilla swirl ice cream that she barely touched and I was working on a cup of peppermint mocha vanilla swirl.

This should have been a romantic part of our date, but something was wrong.

Something had changed. I wasn't sure exactly when it happened, but it happened sometime after we left the restaurant. While we were walking downtown.

She wasn't even looking at me. She was staring into her ice cream, swirling her spoon around the edges. When she saw me looking at her, she took a bite and smiled at me.

But something was off. It was her eyes. She was looking at me as though she was trying to figure something out.

Was she mad at me for kissing her in the restaurant? I had gotten a little carried away, but she hadn't protested. She'd kissed me back just as much as I'd kissed her.

"What's wrong?" I asked.

"Nothing," she said with a little smile. "This is good ice cream."

"Are you sure?"

"Too much lobster," she said.

I nodded. It was a plausible excuse, but I didn't really believe it. Her gaze only met mine for an instant before she looked away again.

"You're still leaving tomorrow afternoon?" I asked.

"I'm not sure," she said. "I need to check with the office."

"We can still go for that hike in the morning."

"Maybe."

Then she set down her spoon and pushed her ice cream aside.

"I'm not feeling very well," she said. "I need to go back to the hotel and lie down for a while."

"Are you sick? Is there anything I can do?"

She shook her head. "It's just a migraine. The elevation, I think."

"It takes a while to get adjusted to the elevation," I said with relief that it wasn't anything serious. I was also feeling relief that she was struggling with the elevation and it wasn't something personal. For her to suddenly go distant like this was troubling.

"Thank you for the ice cream," she said, standing up to go.

"Of course." I took both our bowls and dumped them. She was already headed toward the door.

The saloon was just down a little ways down and across the street from the ice cream shop.

She walked with her hands in her pockets.

"I'm sorry," she said when we reached the stairs leading upstairs in the saloon.

"It's okay," I said. "Just feel better."

She nodded and turned, practically jogging up the stairs.

I was at a loss.

Something had happened.

I just didn't know what it was.

39

BROOKLYN

I closed the door to my room and leaned against the wood.

I was going to be sick. Pushing off from the door, I walked to the window and caught sight of Benjamin walking down the sidewalk.

He'd been so sweet. I'd left my flowers somewhere. In the restaurant, I think.

I'd made the cardinal mistake when I told him who I was. That I was the granddaughter of a multi-billionaire.

I had mistakenly thought it was safe. He knew my family. He knew my grandfather.

He was a successful author. I didn't know too much about having a career in writing, but I was pretty sure that writers weren't wealthy. I'd met a lot of wealthy people at charity functions and such and not one of them was a writer.

Benjamin had a little cabin here in Whiskey Springs and a place in Houston. I hadn't seen either one of them. For all I knew, he spent all his money on flying private.

There were people like that.

I'd been okay with everything. I didn't care how much money he had or didn't have.

That didn't concern me one way or the other.

I liked him. Everything about him.

But then he'd called me an investment. Not in so many words, but close enough for me to catch it.

It was important for someone to like me just for being me.

I had taken a job as a stewardess on a commercial airline in order to maintain my own identity. I was a Worthington through and through and proud of it, but I was also me.

People knew me as Brooklyn Johnson. Just a regular girl working a regular job.

If Benjamin was looking at me as an investment, then I couldn't do it. I couldn't be with someone who only wanted me because I was one of many heirs to Skye Travels.

We'd all been taught since we started dating to be cautious about that.

And, I admit, that caution was probably why I was still single.

I changed into my night clothes, climbed into bed, and stared at the ceiling.

This was what happened when I started breaking my own rules.

Rules were there for a reason.

I didn't date pilots or passengers.

I'd made an exception.

I'd fallen hard for him.

But I had to let him go.

I couldn't be someone's investment.

Now I understood why Grandma advised me to leave things alone.

She knew that some things that were pushed often weren't right.

I'd met Benjamin three times by chance.

First time is chance…

Second time is happenstance…

Third time is fate.

I don't know where'd I'd heard that but it was time to ratify a new rule.

Don't live life according to folklore.

40

BENJAMIN

I spent the next two weeks in my cabin. I decided that I could be a hermit without much trouble.

I chopped firewood. I changed out the sink faucet. I installed a Nest thermostat.

And I wrote. I wrote a lot. I finished the first draft of my novel.

When I had texted Brooklyn the next morning, she sent back a short text telling me that she was on a plane heading back to Houston. Change of plans, she'd said.

I balanced a chunk of wood on a stump, lifted the axe, and sliced it deftly down the middle, splitting the wood into two pieces.

It was going to snow. Tonight, if I was any judge.

I'd been waiting for the first snowfall. Promised myself that after the first snowfall, I could head back to Houston. I wasn't equipped for spending a winter in the mountains. A born and bred southern boy had no business even trying.

Taking a break, I sat on the back steps of my cabin and checked my messages.

My last text to Brooklyn sat there unanswered. Mocking me.

> Text me when you want to talk. I'm here.

I typed a hundred other messages, but I hadn't sent any of them. I'd deleted every one.

I left her alone.

Something had changed for her. I might not ever know what it was.

But I was not a stalker.

She would need to get in touch with me. The ball was in her court.

Anytime I contemplated contacting her, I purposely got busy doing something else.

I was quite productive.

I went inside, showered, and started getting the cabin ready to be left for the winter. I had a checklist of things that needed to be done. Drain the water. Take out the garbage.

Those were things that had to wait until the morning I was ready to go.

But I went ahead and cleaned out the refrigerator. Threw out everything that wouldn't keep until next spring—which was pretty much everything.

And the whole time I thought about Brooklyn.

My sister had even asked about her. That had not been a fun conversation. But to her credit, Analise had not pushed me on an explanation or details. She was a decent sister. Still trying to give me one of her twins, though. She sounded just about at her wit's end and from the crying I heard in the background, I understood.

I spent a lot of time trying to figure out what was wrong with me. Falling for a perfect stranger like that. Was I that desperate for female companionship?

I played around on one of the dating apps until I felt sick to my stomach, then gave up and went back to writing.

I didn't want to date anyone. I wanted to date Brooklyn.

I wanted to do more than date her.

I wanted to make a life with her.

But something had happened.

And from the looks of things, I might not ever know what that something was.

41

BROOKLYN

"𝒫repare for landing."

I sat down in my jump seat, fastened my seat belt, and pressed my head firmly against the back of the seat. Hands under thighs. Standard brace position.

I had volunteered for overtime and that overtime had kept me out of Houston for two weeks. But now I had a mandatory four days off. Company policy.

I wasn't tired. I was just... unhappy.

My smiles had been forced for most of the two weeks.

All in all, I just had not been myself since Whiskey Springs.

Benjamin had somehow slipped beneath my guard and gotten into my heart.

And now I missed him.

I longed to spend time with him again.

To find out what his sister was doing with her twins. I still smiled when I thought about how she'd tried to give him one of her babies.

And then he'd gone and brought me flowers at the airport. The two women, Caroline and Betty, could not have been more happy for me if he'd been there to propose.

I suppose I felt the same way.

My visions of growing old had started to include him.

Family gatherings. Trips. Maybe even a baby of our own.

Hopefully not twins.

But I needed him—anybody—to like me for me and not for my family and the lifestyle they had to offer.

I'd composed a few text messages to Benjamin, but I'd deleted them.

He'd sent me a message that morning.

BENJAMIN

Let me know when you want to talk. I'm here.

I took that to mean that the ball was in my court.

Well, as far as I could tell, it was game over.

I couldn't take the risk of anything else.

The pilot took the plane in for a landing. It was a rather bumpy landing. That told me that the copilot had taken his turn at landing.

I could always tell when the ones with less experience did the takeoffs or the landings.

In the air, it was harder to tell.

"Welcome to Houston," the pilot announced.

My heart tripped like it always did when I got home.

This was the longest I'd been away at any one time since college.

It was still early and it was Saturday.

I'd go home, change, and drive out to Memorial Drive to visit my grandmother.

But I'd check the mailbox first. See if the paperwork for the business had come through.

Richard and I had named our company Skye Angels. It had been my idea and since the company was basically all my idea, he went along with it.

As we taxied down the runway heading for our gate, my cell

phone messages populated. One was a text from Grandma asking me to come by her house as soon as I could.

> Is everything okay?

GRANDMA

I just need your help with something.

> Just landing. It'll be a couple of hours before I can get there.

Somehow I had a feeling she already knew this. She always seemed to know where her children and grandchildren were at any given point. I sometimes wondered if she had some kind of spreadsheet in her head.

She probably had a system like I did for remembering which passengers were sitting where.

At least I didn't have to go to my house and be alone. I'd been alone enough these two weeks. My plan to stay busy had rather backfired on me. I'd ended up spending too many nights alone in hotel rooms.

I'd tortured myself even further by reading three of Grayson Benjamin's books.

It was torture because I could hear his voice in his written words.

My brain was on some kind of loop. No matter what I thought about, I ended up thinking about Benjamin.

42

BENJAMIN

I managed to avoid most social events; however, despite my propensity to be a hermit, I was not a complete recluse.

Tonight was one of those nights that I had to put on a tuxedo with tails, call a driver, and be sociable. It was the one social event a year that my editor insisted I attend. Whatever funds were raised, my publishing house matched dollar for dollar. And I was their representative.

It was the Houston Adult Literacy Gala Ball held at the Houston Museum of Fine Arts and it was tonight.

It was a big event in the world of literacy on both sides—those who donated and those who were on the receiving end.

I couldn't imagine that there were still people who couldn't read. If people showed up and donated to the cause because I was there, then it was well worth the time and effort it took out of my evening.

My driver pulled up to the door and let me out. There were hundreds of people here, all dressed in white tie attire. The men wore white bow ties and white waistcoats. Some even went so far as to wear white gloves and a top hat. It was quite possibly a bit over the top, but this was Houston, Texas and as they said, everything in Texas was bigger.

The concierge at the door handed me a white silk mask to wear over my eyes.

"I hadn't realized tonight was a masked ball," I said.

"A last minute addition to the theme," he said.

The theme was 1920s Glamour, so the masks were an ingenuous addition. The masks for the men had an elastic back and those for the ladies tied at the back.

I took a minute to slip on my mask before I entered the ball room.

An orchestra, also dressed in white tie, sat on one end of the room, their professional classical music providing background for the muted conversations.

Blending into this high society world came natural to me. Maybe because I set so many of my books in this world. Or maybe because both my parents had been attorneys in Savannah. If they attended events like this, they never said, but they could have easily done so.

I took an offered glass of champagne from one of the servers and walked around looking at some of the artwork done by local artists just for this event.

They took some of the event's featured novels, including one of mine, and did a painting to represent it.

Even though this was the first time I had seen it, I recognized it immediately. It was representation of my book *On the Edge of Danger*. The artist had captured not only the full moon spilling over the little cabin in the forest, but also the mood of danger and suspense.

This was one of those nights when I would have liked to have a companion with me. To share this moment. A wife or a girlfriend.

Brooklyn.

But instead, I had no woman on my arm.

I could have easily done so, but I couldn't bear the thought of spending an evening with anyone other than her.

Such was the way of the heart.

I was acutely aware that I was one of the few people who had come alone. Or even if they hadn't come alone they had already found someone to spend the evening with. Since this was a gala, there was waltzing and it had already started.

I gravitated toward the refreshment table, since I had nothing else to do at the moment. I stood there, debating on whether I should have a blueberry canapé or a dark chocolate covered strawberry when I saw a woman in a red dress standing across the room next to an older woman wearing a black dress.

With the masks, it was hard to tell much about who people were, in theory, at least. But I could tell the woman in the black dress was older.

There was something familiar about the woman in the red dress. Something that had my heart pounding in my chest.

I left the refreshment table untouched and slowly circled the room, avoiding the dancers.

If I was right, then this changed everything about tonight.

Maybe even changed everything about everything.

43

BROOKLYN

*T*here wasn't anything I wouldn't do for my Grandma Savannah.

She had summoned me to her house just so I could accompany her to The Houston Adult Literacy Gala Ball, one of her all-time favorite annual events.

Grandpa Noah was going to be there, but his flight was running late and Grandma didn't want to go alone.

I'd never actually been to this particular charity event, so I was curious enough to be a little excited about going. My newfound interest in books and reading probably had something to do with that.

My grandmother, obviously knowing that I would agree to accompany her to this charity event, had arranged to have a ballgown delivered to her house.

The dress she had chosen was a floor length red silk dress. Tasteful décolletage. Bare shoulders. The skirt had miles and miles of material that swirled prettily when I moved.

"It's beautiful," I'd said when Grandma had proudly shown me this perfect ballgown. "I don't have shoes to go with this."

"It's a good thing we wear the same size then," she said, holding up a pair of strappy, sparkly red shoes.

As I got dressed, I thought about how my grandmother was like a fairly Godmother.

But there would be no prince at the ball for me to fall in love with and there would be no clock striking Midnight.

I'd already fallen in love with someone. Someone who had chosen me for the wrong reasons.

Perhaps, I decided as I studied my reflection in the full-length mirror in my grandmother's dressing room, tonight was a good night for me to start over.

The men at this event would not be passengers or pilots, so they were all within the parameters of men I could date.

Grandma wore a stately black ballgown. Before heading out to the car, we took a moment to stand side by side in front of the mirror.

"We could be sisters," I said.

"We could," she said. "if not for the years. But I'm happy." She gave me quick hug. "I hope you find the happiness I've found in my life."

"I hope so, too." But I wasn't so optimistic as she about that.

My heart had been indelibly stamped by Benjamin and it would be a long time before I'd let another man have access to my heartstrings.

We made it to the venue without incident. Grandma's chauffeur, Peter, drove while Grandma talked to Grandpa on the phone. Grandpa had just landed, earlier than he'd thought, and was leaving the airport now.

"You didn't need me, after all," I told her after she disconnected the call.

"It'll do you good," she said.

Then we were there and Peter opened my door before I could ask her what she meant by that. With my grandmother, it could mean just about anything or nothing at all.

We must have arrived fashionably late. People were already waltzing in the ballroom. The orchestra was currently playing the classic Blue Danube by Strauss.

Men wearing formal tuxes and ladies in colorful ballgowns swirled around the room in an array of color.

"I can see why you like this gala so much," I said.

"It's one of the most formal ones," she said.

The concierge rushed up from behind us.

"Pardon me," he said. "Here are your masks."

"It's a masquerade ball?" I asked, taking the white lacy mask from the concierge.

"Apparently so," Grandma said.

"Aren't you on the committee?"

"I am," she said, turning so I could tie her mask in the back. Then she did the same for me. "I think I heard someone mention the idea."

"How will you recognize Grandpa?" I asked.

She put a hand on my arm. "A woman always recognizes her soulmate," she said. "You'll see."

44

BENJAMIN

*M*y stealthy route around the ballroom, avoiding the dancers, was intercepted about halfway around, near the room with the art displays.

Although he wore a black mask like mine, I recognized him immediately. I recognized the way he held himself, tall and straight. His silver, perfectly trimmed silver hair. His voice.

"Hello Benjamin," he said. How he recognized me was a mystery. My only explanation was that Noah Worthington knew everything.

Did he know what had happed to frighten his granddaughter away from me?

"Mr. Worthington," I said. "It's good to see you."

"You too. It's my understanding that you're being honored tonight."

"Honored?" He was mistaken. "No sir. I'm here as a guest."

"I see," he said, then let the topic drop. "Have you seen my wife?"

"I don't know," I said. "The masks…"

"Right."

I didn't bother to tell him that I had never met his wife, so even without the masks, I wouldn't know whether I had seen her. He seemed preoccupied.

He clapped me on the shoulder. "Congratulations," he said.

"For what?" I asked, but he was already walking away, supposedly searching for his wife. Noah seemed to be confused. He thought I was being honored at this event, but I was just one of many here tonight representing the cause for literacy.

Putting Noah and his confusion—perhaps he was getting older—out of my mind, I continued my way around the dance floor in my quest to reach the girl in red.

Standing just a few feet from her, now, I knew I was right. It didn't matter that she was wearing a mask, or that I could only see her profile. I knew who she was.

The girl in red was Brooklyn. Brooklyn was here. She was the lady in red.

She sensed me watching her and turned to face me.

It only took a second before I saw the flicker of recognition in her eyes.

Determined not to miss this moment, I stepped forward and held out a gloved hand.

"May I have this dance?"

She glanced over at the lady in the black ballgown standing next to her.

I immediately saw the resemblance between the two women and put it all together. She was Noah's wife and Brooklyn's grandmother.

"Do you mind if I borrow her?" I asked Mrs. Worthington. She merely smiled and shrugged a little.

Brooklyn put her hand in mine. She, too, wore white gloves, but hers continued all the way up over her elbows. Her shoulders were bare. No jewelry, but she didn't need any. She was the most lovely woman here.

I could feel the warmth of her hand even through my glove and hers.

"Why are you here?" she asked as I led her out to the dance floor.

"It's a worthy charity," I said.

"I agree," she said just before I took her for a spin.

She was breathless by the time I slowed down again as the music changed.

"Have you seen my painting?" I asked.

"You paint?"

"Funny. The painting is by a local artist based on one of my books."

"I'd like to see it," she said.

I took her hand and led her off the dance floor toward the painting display room.

"Can you guess which one is mine?" I asked. There were a dozen paintings along the walls.

A person would have to have read my book *On the Edge of Danger* to recognize it.

She walked right up to mine. "This one," she said. "The artist captured the danger. The little cabin and the full moon."

She turned and looked at me. "Is this your cabin?"

I didn't know whether I was supposed to laugh or not.

"God. I hope not," I said.

45

BROOKLYN

*A*bout the time Grandpa caught up with Grandma, I turned around to go in search of the refreshment table and came face to face with Benjamin.

I'd known him instantly. My grandmother's words were right there.

A woman always recognizes her soulmate. You'll see.

And I did see.

When he held out his hand and led me onto the dance floor, I forgot all about my concerns with him. He obviously was a man of many talents, formal dancing included.

At the moment, any concerns I'd had didn't seem to matter anymore.

All that mattered while he deftly swept me around the ballroom was the way he looked at me with his deep blue eyes with traces of violet. He looked at me like I was the only person in the world.

Since I'd been reading his books, it wasn't hard for me to recognize the painting that had been done to represent his book, *The Edge of Danger*. It wasn't his latest book, but it was still on the bestseller list and I had already read it.

"I love this painting," I said. "It captures the feel of your books. Not just *The Edge of Danger.*"

"You really like it?"

"I really do. The light in the cabin window offsets the danger."

"I didn't even notice the light in the cabin window."

He smiled at me and the past two weeks vanished.

"I missed you," he said softly.

"I missed you, too." I swallowed the lump in my throat. I'd tried so hard not to think about him. And I had been so terribly unsuccessful. Maybe it didn't matter that he saw me as some kind of investment. It didn't mean that he couldn't love me.

He swept a strand of hair off my face. "You're beautiful," he said.

"You're handsome in your tuxedo."

"They're taking photos down the hall. Would you do me the honor of having your photograph taken with me?"

"Yes," I said, simply.

A few minutes later, we stood in front of a photographer with a very thick Mexican accent.

"You make very nice couple," he said. "Very happy."

I started to shake my head. To clarify that we weren't actually a couple, but Benjamin squeezed my hand.

"Thank you," he said. "We are very happy."

"You pick up photos in dos hours," he said, holding up two fingers.

"I guess we'll be here for two more hours," I said.

"Is that so bad?"

The music changed back to waltzing music.

"No," I said, looking into his eyes. He was the most handsome man here tonight, excluding my grandfather, of course. It be would weird to compare the two of them.

"I need to run a quick errand," Benjamin said. "Will you wait for me?"

"I'll wait right over here," I said, waving my hand toward an unoccupied bench in a quiet area.

I sat on the bench and arranged my skirts around me.

I wondered what kind of errand Benjamin might need to run at a gala, but since he had a painting to showcase his books, he could easily have some kind of business to take care of.

Anyway, it gave me a minute to catch my breath.

Benjamin was a whirlwind tonight, leaving me breathless. But he did that to me. I took a deep breath to steady my heart rate and straightened my gloves. My grandmother had done an incredible job of putting together my dress and accessories for tonight.

It was almost like she'd known Benjamin would be here.

The thought gave me pause. She was on the committee. She would know.

Of course she'd known.

I'd had no idea Grandma Savannah was so cunning.

46
———

BENJAMIN

*B*y the time I took care of my business, just under the deadline, and made my way back to Brooklyn, the ceremony was starting.

We went along with the crowd to the grand ballroom. The music had stopped and two emcees stood at a podium at the front of the room.

"Good evening," the older of the two said into the microphone. "To get things started, you may remove your masks."

I reached up and swept my mask off while Brooklyn reached back to untie hers.

"Can I help?" I asked.

"Yes. Thank you."

There was something oddly intimate about pulling the string to release her mask.

And now, seeing her without it, my heart felt like it was going to burst out of sheer happiness. I loved looking at her. Just looking at her.

"Now," the emcee said. "Let's talk about the auctions."

Someone brought one of the paintings around and set it on a stand at the front of the room next to the speakers.

"They auctioned the paintings?" Brooklyn asked.

"A silent auction," I said.

She looked vexed.

"What?"

"I wish I had known."

"Why is that?" I asked.

"I would have bid on yours."

"I don't think you want to do that," I said.

She elbowed me. "I liked it."

"Really? Enough to put on your wall?"

"Absolutely."

"Well then." I leaned back on my heels and tried not to look smug.

Brooklyn liked the painting. I wasn't sure I'd completely believed her earlier, but now I did.

"This painting went for $500,000 to Mr. George Brown." The emcee announced.

"$500,000?" Brooklyn repeated. "I see now why it's white tie."

"Indeed," I said, then leaned close. "And they start with the lowest one."

"This should be interesting," she said.

I agreed completely. Things could get very interesting.

When servers came around carrying trays of sparkling champagne, I grabbed two and handed one to Brooklyn.

One by one, the paintings were brought around and the highest bidder was announced. Each time the bidding went up by at $100,000.

By the time the ninth painting was brought out, the amount was up to one million.

And mine still had not come out.

"Let's take a break, folks," the emcee said. "Give the excitement time to build at bit."

"I don't know how much more exciting it can get," Brooklyn said.

"Want to step outside, get some fresh air?"

"Okay," she said and off we went, through the French doors, to the outside garden with fragrant magnolia blossoms filling the air.

"It's not as pretty as Colorado, is it?" she asked.

"It's pretty in its own charming way," I said.

For me the most beautiful place in the world was anyplace Brooklyn was.

47

BROOKLYN

*D*uring the break, a team of workers brought out chairs. It seems someone on the committee figured out that standing for so long was taxing on many people.

Benjamin and I found a couple of vacant chairs near the back and sat down. My red strappy shoes were pretty, but my feet were starting to ache.

"Everyone ready to get started again?" the emcee asked.

There was a round of applause.

"Do you think yours will be last?" I asked, feeling a tingling of excitement.

He shook his head. "I don't know. Maybe."

"It's already a successful fundraiser," I said, mostly to myself.

"And now we're going to bring out the last three together," the emcee announced.

Three young men brought the last three paintings out and set them on the display easels.

"Anyone care to make a wager?" he asked.

A lot of laughter followed, but no one dared to bet on any of the paintings.

They were all nice. Benjamin's had the darkest mood, but that matched his books. There was one that looked like a western, and there was one that was obviously a contemporary romance.

It was down to these three.

"You'll win," I said, leaning over.

"I'm not sure it's a competition like that. No one knows what anyone else bid."

"Hm."

The next one up was the contemporary romance. I nudged Benjamin's arm.

"Told you."

"There are two left."

"They're up to almost two million."

I had to admit, it was a lot of money for a painting by a local artist.

"Do the artists get anything?" I asked.

"I don't know. I think they donate them. It's a discoverability thing."

"I see."

"And now," the emcee said. "the second highest goes to… the contemporary western one."

"You won," I said.

"Someone did," he said.

"What do you mean?"

"We still don't know who the highest bidder is."

"True," I said, although I wasn't quite sure what that had to do with anything. From what I could see, someone had bid a lot of money to get a painting that represented Benjamin's books. That had to be good discoverability for his books as well as the artist.

I was lost in my thoughts when I heard the emcee move to the final painting.

"This one represents the books of Benjamin Gray writing as

Grayson Benjamin." He paused. "He gave us permission to reveal his real name."

The emcee pulled out the last index card and looked at it. "Wow," he said.

The audience was quiet as everyone waited for him to share the results.

"Tell us how much," someone said.

"You all ready for this?"

The groans of impatience were answer enough.

"Three million five hundred."

Clapping. Everyone clapped.

I watched Benjamin. He sat very still. Still and straight. No expression.

"And the donor is…" He stopped and looked out at the audience. "The donor wants to remain anonymous, but the painting goes to Brooklyn Johnson."

I looked around, my own name not sinking in.

Benjamin nudged me. "Go," he said. "It's yours."

"No," I said. "I didn't bid."

"It's a gift."

I shook my head even as I stood up.

"Come with me," I said, grabbing his hand.

In my haze of disbelief it made perfect since that he, as the writer should be recognized, too.

48

BENJAMIN

*B*rooklyn and I danced until she declared that her feet couldn't go another step in her heels.

Noah and Savannah found us sitting on a bench in a quiet alcove just before eleven o'clock.

Savannah sat next to her granddaughter.

"I recognize that look," she said. "It's the shoes."

"They're beautiful," Brooklyn said. "but they aren't for dancing."

"Trade with me," Savannah said.

"Oh no—" But Savannah had already slipped out of her shoes.

Brooklyn had to unbuckled hers, so it took a few minutes longer.

"Congratulations," Noah said, holding out a hand.

"I didn't really do anything."

Noah narrowed his eyes at me, but refrained from further comment.

Minutes later, Brooklyn and Savannah were wearing each other's shoes.

"We came to tell you that we're leaving," Savannah said.

Brooklyn glanced at me. "I 'um. I rode with my grandmother."

"I'll get you home," I said, then turned to her grandparents. "Don't worry. I have a car and driver."

"Have fun," Savannah said, leaning forward to kiss Brooklyn on the cheek.

"Are you sure?" she asked me after they left. "I don't want to inconvenience you."

I didn't even bother with a response.

"I need to find out who bought the painting." She said. "I really can't accept it."

"Well," I said. "You can't refuse it."

"Give me one good reason why not."

I leaned back and considered which one of many reasons I wanted to give her.

"It would be an insult," I said, choosing that one that seemed like the worst.

She narrowed her eyes at me. "Then he or she should make himself known. Otherwise I might think he'll want something in return."

"Okay," I said. "That's a good point. But what if it was someone like your grandfather?"

"He would tell me." She sounded so sure of that.

"We will have to agree to disagree on this particular topic. Just sleep on it, okay?"

She nodded. She really had no choice. The painting was in her stewardship at the moment and she couldn't just leave it here.

"How are your feet?" I asked, glancing down.

"Much better. But I won't be dancing tonight."

"That's unfortunate," I said. "You want to get out of here?"

There would be dancing until Midnight, but since we wouldn't be doing it, we had no reason to stay here.

"Yes," she said.

"Wait here," I said. "I'll make sure they have your painting wrapped and ready to go."

"And our photos," she said. "They should be ready."

"I won't be long."

49

BROOKLYN

"*I* can go with—" I started to stand up, but even with different shoes, my feet had had it for the night.

He smiled. "Really. I won't be long."

As I walked off, I blew out a breath and realized that I was exhausted. My day had started at four a.m. and now it was pushing Midnight.

What I needed most right now was sleep.

I certainly didn't need a three and half million-dollar painting.

My grandfather would not spend that much on a painting. But it wasn't about the painting, I reminded myself. It was about the charity.

The music was wonderful and it would have been nice to dance with him again. I replayed our dance in my head and that sent me back to that kiss that had gotten us into so much trouble.

"The painting is in the car," Benjamin said, coming back. "Along with the photos."

"Are you cold?" he asked.

"Yes." I hadn't even realized I had been rubbing my arms.

"Here," he said, taking off his tuxedo jacket and helping me into it.

It was huge on me, the sleeves covering my hands. There was something oddly intimate about wearing his jacket.

For one, it smelled like him. Like ink and spice. Maybe vanilla.

As we skirted our way around the dance floor to the front entrance, it was a good feeling knowing that everyone knew that we were leaving together. I wanted everyone to know that we were together.

I liked being with Benjamin.

When I put a hand on his arm, he smiled at me.

I'd been so stupid to just walk away from him.

But even now there was that little nagging doubt in the back of my mind. I wanted it to just go away. To be forgotten. But caution had been hounded into me for my entire life.

The night air was cold and I was grateful I had his jacket.

We stood at the curb and waited for Benjamin's driver to bring the car back around. He'd had to make a loop around while he waited for us.

"Are you okay?" he asked.

"Yes."

"Mr. Gray," an older man called out. "Can I speak to you about something?"

"Go ahead," I said. "I'll be okay."

"I won't be long."

Without him standing next to me to break the wind, it was decidedly colder.

Since the tuxedo had no pockets, I pulled it tighter around me.

As I did, I discovered a secret pocket just on the inside. A tuxedo was not supposed to have pockets.

Curious, I ran my fingers along the inside of the pocket just to see how big it was. Was it big enough for a cell phone? I quickly discovered that it was not. But there was a square of folded paper there.

Still maintaining that tuxedo jackets were not supposed to have pockets, I pulled out the piece of paper. If this was a rented tuxedo, it could be a secret map or a lost love letter or anything.

I pulled it out and carefully unfolded the piece of paper.

It was not a secret map or a lost love letter. It was a receipt.

A receipt with Benjamin Gray's name on it. Paid in full printed in bold letters.

It was a receipt for a three and a half million-dollar painting.

With a glance in his direction, I frantically refolded the receipt and stuffed it back where I had found it.

Benjamin, his back still to me, looked over his shoulder and held up a finger, indicating he needed one more minute.

I nodded as expected, but my mind raced. It probably wasn't even a rented tuxedo anyway. I shouldn't have looked at the paper. But I had.

Benjamin had bought the painting for his own book. Nothing wrong with that.

But there might something wrong about paying that much money for it.

For charity.

If not that, then there had to be something wrong with him buying it and gifting it to me. And secretly.

It seemed to me that a man who spent that kind of money on a gift would want some kind of credit for it. Some recognition.

I looked back at Benjamin.

He was so handsome even just in his white shirt without his jacket. Surely he was cold, but he showed no sign of it.

This was a classic case of when knowing was far worse than not knowing.

50

BENJAMIN

*M*r. White had wanted to talk to me about a book signing at his next event.

I told him I would talk to my editor. But then he wanted me to meet his wife who apparently was a big fan of my books.

As I smiled and nodded, I was reminded of why I preferred to be a semi-hermit.

Semi because right now I didn't want to be alone, I wanted to be with Brooklyn.

"I really have to go," I said, finally. "My car is here and my date is waiting."

They apologized and promised to see me at the next event.

I didn't tell them I rarely did events of any kind.

"I'm so sorry," I said when I reached Brooklyn's side again.

"It's okay," she said. "Famous author and all."

"That never happens," I said. "But unfortunately, tonight you made sure everyone knew who I was," I said, teasingly.

"It can be a good thing," she said as the driver opened the door for her and she stepped inside. I slid in next to her.

As the driver pulled out onto the road, she looked over at me.

"Don't you want some recognition for what you do?"

"I guess a little is okay. But mostly I do it because I enjoy the process of writing and I like getting paid for what I love to do."

"Hm." We sat in silence until the driver merged onto the freeway.

"So this person," she said. "the one who bought the painting and gave it to me. Doesn't it seem strange that someone would do that?"

"It doesn't seem strange to me. To me it's just giving money to charity. The painting is just something tangible to get in exchange."

She nodded. It appeared that she wasn't going to let this go easily. It was a lot of money, but I'd had an inside tip that the only way I was going to be walking out with it was to bid extremely high.

Since I always donated to literacy anyway, it didn't seem like such a stretch.

"Maybe you should let it go."

"Maybe," she said. "I haven't decided yet."

I wasn't sure exactly what that meant, but it was past time to change the subject.

"So…" I said with a little sideways smile. "We can't get kicked out of my car own car."

She looked up at me with a matching smile.

"What are you trying to say?"

"I'm just saying."

"Benjamin Gray," she said. "You are incorrigible."

"Part of my charm," I said, taking her hand.

Pulling her close, I kissed her on the cheek, then her eyelids, then the corner of her mouth.

As she turned to me, our lips met.

I forgot about the traffic. I forgot about the driver. I had only one thought in my head.

I could kiss this girl every minute for the rest of my life.

51

<hr/>

BROOKLYN

*B*enjamin held my hand as we walked from the driveway toward the door of my patio home.

It had been a magical evening, notwithstanding my feet that ached with every step.

"Your driver must be tired of waiting," I said.

"He thinks nothing of it," Benjamin said.

"That's a rather odd statement," I said, grinning at him.

"When can I see you again?" Benjamin asked as I keyed in the code that let me into the gate of my patio home.

Instead of opening it, leaned back against the iron bars. "I don't know. What are you thinking?"

"I was thinking maybe we could have dinner tomorrow," he said, running a finger lightly across my cheek.

"I'll have to check my schedule."

"You're that busy, huh?" He lightly kissed me on my already swollen lips.

"I can be free tomorrow night."

"Yeah?" He kissed my top lip and I closed my eyes.

"I think so. Yes."

"I should go then. So you can get some sleep."

I nodded.

He swung open the gate and as we reached my door, the motion light came on.

"Arg." I put a hand over my eyes.

He leaned against the door. "Pick you up tomorrow at seven?"

"Okay." Then I remembered that I was still wearing his jacket. "I need to give you this."

"I think we forgot something else," he said as he helped me out of his jacket.

"What?" I asked, my brain still hazy from his kisses.

"We left something in the car."

"The painting." I bit my lip. How could we have forgotten about a three and a half million-dollar painting? "And our photos."

"I'll be right back."

I opened the door and, stepping inside out of the cold, watched for Benjamin through the glass.

"Where do you want to put it?" he asked, with a quick glance around, holding the painting carefully by the edges.

"In my reading nook," I said.

"You have a reading nook?" he asked.

"Of course."

"If I ever had any question that you were the perfect girl for me…"

I cut my eyes at him.

My reading nook was a little alcove off the main living room, lined with books on one side and a comfortable chaise in the middle, a reading lamp behind it. The big windows on one wall caught the morning light, giving me a view of the patio part of my patio home, mostly grass that someone moved every Tuesday, a tall stone fence giving me privacy.

A little gas fireplace on the opposite wall from the bookcases had nothing on the wall over it.

"There," I said, pointing to that empty wall.

He propped the painting on the mantle.

"It's like you were saving a place for it."

The painting did look like it had been made specifically for me and my reading nook.

"I guess maybe I was." I looked at him, wondering...

"What is it?" he asked.

"What did you mean when you said I was an investment?"

"When did I say that?"

"In Whiskey Springs. You said I was an investment."

"I don't remember that, but you are," he said. "You're my future."

"Your future." Those two words settled over me like a soothing balm that at the same time sent anticipatory tingles all through me.

"If you want to be," he said, pulling me close against him and running a finger lightly over my lips.

I looked into his sky-blue eyes with hints of lavender and knew that there was nothing I wanted more than to be his future.

"I want to be," I said, my words coming out in a whisper.

He kissed me again, cupping the back of my head with the palm of his hand.

Grandma Savannah had been right. Things worked out the way they were supposed to.

And what seemed like chance probably wasn't chance at all.

EPILOGUE
BROOKLYN

Six months later

I swirled around in my chair and watched one of the Skye Travels private jets come in for a landing.

My office in the Skye Travels office building gave me a clear view of the airport runways.

That was the thing about my grandfather's company, I mused. It had a tendency to pull us back to it like a magnetic beacon.

I didn't work for Skye Travels, but I had an office there. It just made sense.

Over the months, Richard and I had worked out a system that worked well for us.

His focus was on doing the paperwork and I worked face to face with our people.

Skye Angels had started off slow, purposely, but it was going well enough now that I had resigned from being a stewardess.

Now I supervised the stewardesses—flight attendants—who contracted out to work on private flights. It was a need that

Grandpa had filled sporadically, but he'd never set up any specific system.

Skye Angels filled that need.

I watched the plane as it taxied along the tarmac.

Ten minutes later, the door opened and the stairs were slowly lowered.

Uncle Dylan came to the door first, then stepped aside.

Benjamin came to the door next. He was holding a baby on his hip. As he carefully stepped down, his sister followed, also with a baby.

Benjamin had left this morning to fly to Boston to bring his sister and her babies for a visit. Her husband was traveling this week for work, so the timing was perfect.

I left my desk and was downstairs and out the back door before they got across the tarmac.

Benjamin leaned over to kiss me.

"Is this one ours?" I whispered, smiling at the little girl dressed prettily in a pink dress. "

Brooklyn?"

"Yes," he said. "Just don't tell Analise." He glanced over his shoulder. "I think she's decided to keep both of them."

"I won't breath a word." Then I turned to Benjamin's sister. "Welcome to Houston."

"Thank you."

"Come inside out of the sun while they unload your luggage."

I could already see that she had brought everything. Car seats and... a crib?

"I hope it's not too much," she said when she saw me looking. "Benjamin said I could bring whatever we needed."

"No need to worry," I said. "I was just trying to imagine what it must be like to have to have two of everything."

"Maybe you'll find out one day," she said, with a pointed look at her brother.

"Just ignore her," Benjamin said. "I'd blame it on motherhood, but she's always been a little messed up in the head."

I laughed.

"Can I hold him?" I asked, looking from Benjamin to his sister.

Benjamin passed the baby over to me.

"So cute," I said. And it felt so right having a baby on my hip, especially one related to Benjamin.

Benjamin held the door as we went inside.

I would tell him after his sister left, I decided.

This visit was about her and his nieces. No need to disrupt their trip with my own news.

By next Christmas Benjamin and I would have our own little baby.

Maybe we'd name her Analise.

Keep Reading for a preview of SEALED WITH A KISS...

PREVIEW SEALED WITH A KISS

Prologue
Amelia

1815

*W*ith the moon no more than a sliver, a scattered array of stars, tossed against the inky sky, were bright tonight.

It was a lovely spring evening, chilly following the warmth of day. One of those evenings when lightning bugs sparkled as they left the ground to make their way into the trees.

Inside her house along the shore of Lake Huron, Amelia moved from the window where other than fireflies, she could saw only the faint glow of the lighthouse across the water.

Pausing to study a painting on the wall, Amelia bit her lip and contemplated whether it should be moved to the other side of the room where she could see it while she drank her tea at breakfast.

The painting was a rather nice likeness of her and her new husband, Carlton.

Carlton was breathtakingly handsome in his British uniform and Amelia looked lovely in her wedding gown. They had been so very young. Barely out of leading strings, they had been consumed with that first blush of love reserved only for the young.

The painting had been done in England, just days after their wedding, and right before Carlton sailed for America. That the painting had survived the voyage was a miracle in and of itself.

Carlton had said he would build her a house and build her a house he did.

He'd come here with the British soldiers to fight in what became known as the War of 1812.

After the capture of Fort Mackinac, Carlton had sworn his allegiance to America and sent for his wife. He built this house while she traveled, but he had been called back before she arrived.

They had been like two ships passing in the night.

She received a letter just two weeks ago that he would be home by the end of June.

The end of June had come and gone.

But Carlton had not returned.

With every knock at the door her heart leapt with hope that it might be Carlton.

But when the knock came tonight after the sun had already set, she knew even before she reached the door that it was not Carlton.

"Hello," she said, opening the door to the soldier waiting on the other side of the door.

He was a kind man, young. Much as Amelia and Carlton

had been when they had wed. After delivering the letter, he had left her alone again.

Taking the letter with her, she went sit on the sofa, the painting on the wall in front of her.

She sat there, holding it in her hands, staring at the images in shadows on the wall. After some time, after the clock chimed the hour, she pulled a candle close and slipped her finger beneath the fold, breaking the wax seal on the envelope. A seal she did not recognize.

Carlton was not coming home. He had been lost at sea.

She sat there, thinking nothing and everything for hours. She didn't cry. She hardly felt anything other than an odd numbness.

It was after the clock struck Midnight and the candle had sputtered out that Amelia managed to drag herself from the couch.

She went to her writing desk, uncorked a bottle of ink, and began to write.

> My dearest Carlton,
> They tell me you were lost at sea.
> But I want you to know that I will never give up on you.
> If there is the remotest chance that you could still be out there somewhere, I will wait for you.
> Know that I will stay here at this house. Until the end of time. And I will wait for you.
> I will wait because true love never dims.
> Your truest love,
> Amelia

LEAVING the letter out for the ink to dry, she dragged herself upstairs and, not even bothering to undress, crawled beneath the blankets.

She didn't wake up.

She died that night of takotsubo syndrome.

A broken heart.

Chapter 1
Bailey Winters

DARK BLUE WATER, lapping against the sandy shore, stretched to the horizon where it blended into a hazy band, then blossomed into a light blue sky with fluffy fair weather cumulus clouds drifting lazily.

A faint glow from the top of the lighthouse just out from the water's edge deferred its warning sentinel to the bright mid-morning sunlight.

Standing at my floor to ceiling living room window, I watched as a ferry, a tall spray of water following in its wake, sailed its way across Lake Huron. The ferry would be packed with early season tourists coming out to spend the day on Mackinac Island. As the ferry neared the island, the mournful wail of its horn echoed across the water.

It was still hard to think of myself as anything other than a tourist.

My living room.

I came from a small family. No siblings. No cousins. My mother's older sister, Aunt Meagan, never married, but she'd knocked her career out of the park.

Started her own marketing company. Worked freelance. Made a stellar reputation for herself.

I visited her often in the summers when I was in high school. She'd spent a little time with me, but mostly she worked. She'd always made it a point to spend a few hours every afternoon with me, an early dinner, then she'd park me in front of the television and go back to her computer.

Sometimes I would slip out and walk down the sidewalk along the shore to downtown Mackinac. I'd just sit on a bench and watch people with the fascination of a teenager. I'd wondered what it would be like to be here on this romantic island with a boyfriend. I imagined how we'd get ice cream and watch the sunset.

But Aunt Meagan. She had worked hard. She'd been very successful.

She'd died far too young and as far as I knew, alone.

It was not a happy story for her.

I'd learned from her. I'd learned how to be successful and work hard. But I had also learned the importance of taking time off.

I'd learned, from Aunt Meagan's way of life, the importance of family.

I'd dated, seriously, one guy in college. After we'd split up, I had pretty much avoided relationships. Just because it was my fault, didn't make it hurt any less.

Then just when my life seemed to be settling in for the long haul, Aunt Meagan had gone and left me this house on Mackinac Island.

I was only twenty-six. Too young to live on this island alone. Or so I had thought until I got here.

There was a magic on Mackinac island. I'd always attributed it to the fancifulness of youth. Since I hadn't been here since I was seventeen, I saw it differently through my adult eyes.

Now as an adult, I knew it had not just been my childhood imagination. It really was magical.

Maybe it was the view. Maybe it was the cool air blended with the bright sunshine. Maybe it was the way the tourists carefreely rode their bicycles up and down the path along the lakeshore.

But still, I packed. I packed up a woman's life. A woman who had a successful career. Had she been lonely, I wondered? Or content in her own world?

Holding a roll of packing tape in one hand, I leaned against the window frame and watched an airplane approach the island. It was a small jet. A Cessna.

My college boyfriend, an aviation major, had been into airplanes and had loved to tell me all about them.

I didn't care about airplanes, but I cared that he cared. And whether I had wanted it to or not, information had soaked in. I was like that. A sponge, my father called me.

The ringing of a phone startled me. I checked my cell, but that wasn't it. Then I remembered.

My aunt, oddly enough, still had her landline. The same phone number she'd had for years.

I already fielded a couple of phone calls—that had been unpleasant to say the least.

"Hello?" I always answered my aunt's phone with a question.

There was silence for a moment.

"This is Betty from Houston. Is Meagan available?"

Taking the cordless phone with me, I dropped onto the sofa. I hated, hated doing this. Explaining to people that Aunt Meagan wasn't here anymore. I could say the words now, without emotion. I suppose I had developed some self-protective numbness.

"Give me a minute and I'll call you back," Betty from

Houston, her voice a little hoarse, said after I finished my narrative.

As I sat there waiting for her to call back, I stared at the painting on the wall in front of me. The painting had been here in this same spot for as long as I could remember. It was a faded painting of a young couple. A man in his uniform and a young lady in what I always imagined to be her wedding gown.

Even in the faded black and white painting, I could see the happiness the artist had captured in their eyes.

Five minutes later, Betty from Houston called back.

"Sometimes your aunt rented out her guest room to my employees."

Did I know that? There was a guest room behind the kitchen and now that I thought about it, it was obviously for guests. It hadn't occurred to me to consider what guests.

"I didn't really know that," I said. "Employees?"

"Worthington Enterprises," Betty said. "Not all the time. Just a night or two here and there."

"Okay." While I'd been going my aunt's things, I'd noticed some odd notations that now made sense.

Maybe it was how she kept from being lonely.

At any rate, it was time to tackle Aunt Meagan's financial records. I needed to be sure.

"But I need it for six months this time," Betty said. She named off an amount that left me momentarily speechless.

"We pay ahead and I can transfer the money electronically to your account."

"Okay," I said. The amount would cover my apartment rent in Dallas for at least two years. I gave her my cell phone number that linked to my bank account.

"Great," Betty from Houston said. "I don't know which of my guys it will be yet, but I'll go ahead and send over the money to reserve the room."

Just minutes after we disconnected, I had a notice on my

phone that the full amount she named had just been deposited in my account.

The guest could rent the whole house for that amount. I'd be out of here soon anyway.

NINE DAYS LATER, however, I was still here.

At the time Betty from Dallas had called, I figured I'd rent out the room, put the house on the market, and go back to my life in Dallas.

But I was still here.

And I'd somehow, through the process of setting up my own work area in my aunt's upstairs office, gotten comfortable working here.

I was inspired by the view of the lake that looked more like an ocean. The white birds that dipped down into the water and back up, often times with a fish in their beaks.

Found comfort in watching the neighbor who walked his white Siberian Husky every morning at seven o'clock. And again in the evenings. Sometimes he tossed a stick into the water for the dog to chase after. Sometimes, when it was cold, they would just walk down the sidewalk, then hurry back home to the warmth of their own home.

Maybe it was the horse and buggies, in lieu of automobiles, that passed by on the road below. There were no cars on Mackinac and that had always been something that I found to be enchanting in and of itself.

There were only two ways to get on and off Mackinac Island. By ferry or by airplane.

Chapter 2
Cody Johnson

A TYPICAL WEDNESDAY morning for a flight.

The early morning sun streamed in through the cockpit window on the right, glancing off the computer screens in front of me.

The horizon stretched for miles in every direction, the blue sky blending into land. It looked like an artist had taken a brush and blurred the horizon into a haze so it was hard to tell where the sky stopped and land began. It was as if a molecular reaction occurred, fusing the land and sky together.

It was an optical illusion, of course. But with only the occasional radio chatter coming through my headset, my mind was free to roam.

A perfect day for flying, not a cloud in the sky, with radar assurance that the skies would be clear all the way to my destination.

After adjusting my four-point harness, I set the controls to autopilot.

It was just me floating above the world. No passengers.

I leveled out at ten thousand feet. My favorite altitude. I liked it because for one, it was considered by many, my grandfather included, to be the safest for individual planes of this size.

The second reason was purely personal. The view on the ground at this level still looked human. I could see highways, houses of all sizes, a small-town baseball field. A freight engine snaked its way along the miles and miles of track in what looked like slow motion.

The movement of tiny cars and trains was reminiscent of when I sat at my grandfather's feet playing with my miniature airplanes, flying them high over miniature cars and buildings.

This Phenom 100 was a small jet compared to the others

owned by Skye Travels, but it was smooth, responsive, and comfortable.

What more could one want from an airplane besides smooth and responsive and comfortable? A touch of luxury. Check. Exceptional speed. Check. Lots of cargo storage. Check. My Trek off-road bicycle in a color called rage red fit easily in the storage area in the back with plenty of room left for my luggage and my golf club bag.

I typically traveled light. Nothing more than an overnight bag. But this was a longer trip.

Much longer.

It would have been a typical Wednesday morning.

Except it wasn't.

Only six months.

I could live anywhere for six months. It wasn't long enough to rent an apartment, but it was too long to live in a hotel.

Betty at the office had reserved a room for me. That was all I knew at this point. A room in someone's house.

So I had closed up my twenty-first floor Uptown Houston apartment and asked the concierge to hold my mail.

My job, flying for the prestigious Skye Travels Airline, required me to do whatever was needed. And since I was not only one of the newest hires, but also had no wife and kids, I was recruited to cover for Mike Phillips, a pilot on maternity leave.

I'd met Mike, of course, and considered him to be an admirable fellow.

Notwithstanding Mike's situation, I had to do what was needed to help out the company. That my grandfather, Noah Worthington, was the founder and owner of the company didn't give me more weight. Sometimes it actually seemed like being one of Noah's grandsons gave me more responsibility by default.

Noah had told me when I was younger, before I was even

considering going to work there—not that I hadn't always known that I would—that the company was ours and we had to do whatever it took to make sure it ran smoothly. I hadn't really known what he meant by that at the time, but his words branded themselves into my brain and this particular responsibility seemed to be a perfect illustration.

Another airplane flew in front of me, not close, but just close enough for me to know it was there. Two airships passing in the sky.

One day the sky would be filled with airplanes just as the freeways were filled with cars today. Already, airplanes had autopilot. One day, probably not in my lifetime, they would be as simple to operate as cars, putting most us pilots out of jobs. I imagined that they would be made of some type of metal that, like holding two magnets with like poles close together, would repel each other, preventing the airplanes from running into each other.

Perhaps they should build cars out of that type of metal, too.

My current, not really serious, girlfriend, Charlotte, had not been happy or particularly unhappy about this semi-permanent relocation. I hadn't offered to bring her with me, our relationship wasn't like that, nor had it come up in our brief conversation two days ago. I hadn't seen or talked to her since then. That was one point of relief. I had honestly expected hysterics.

The clear sky had white puffy clouds now, probably coming from the moisture of the great lakes.

I was just thirty minutes out now.

Just a three-hour flight and my life was about to be completely different. Sometimes it took three hours to get from my apartment to the airport north of Houston. Depending on traffic.

As a pilot, travel was part of my life.

That part was nothing new. Just a part of daily life.

But moving to live in a different part of the country... that was something new and unexpected.

Only six months.

Chapter 3
Bailey

Sitting upstairs in my little office, I worked on a marketing plan for a client in Houston.

I'd been at it for three hours and my eyes were starting to cross.

I sat back in what was the most comfortable desk chair I had ever sat in and gazed outside. Aunt Meagan had the best of everything.

The next-door neighbor was walking his Husky, a dog named Bandit, so named because the white dog's fur had what looked like a black mask over his eyes.

The sound of an incoming airplane caught my attention. As I watched, it came close enough for me to see that this plane was a Phenom, probably a Phenom 100 from what I could see from here.

It made a sweep around the island, then went in for what I knew would be a landing.

I'd only lived here for two weeks, but I already knew the patterns and was making some of my own.

In fact, I checked my phone, it was time for me to take my midday break.

I put on my lace up hiking books and grabbed a jacket before I headed outside.

The cool air beneath the bright sunshine still surprised me. Born and bred in Houston, I was accustomed to stepping outside into uncomfortable heat and humidity in the middle of the day.

But not here. Here the sun was warm and the air cool.

I walked down what had quickly become a familiar path down the sidewalk along the shoreline towards town.

Even though it was early in the season, the streets were a little more crowded every day. There was a little sandwich shop on this side of town that I liked for lunch.

Instead of inside dining, it had a walkup window and picnic tables out front. I liked that I was almost always the only customer to sit outside at the tables. Most people got their orders to go.

"Do you want the usual?" the girl behind the counter asked. Her name was Nikki and she always had a smile.

"Yes, please."

Since there was no one behind me, I waited while the cook in the back prepared my chicken burrito.

"You going to stay through the summer?" Nikki asked.

"I don't know for sure," I said. "I still have lots to pack up before I can put the house up for sale."

"I can only imagine," she said, leaning forward with her elbows on the counter. "Your aunt came here a lot, too."

"She did?"

"Sure. It's a quick walk and all."

"It gets kinda lonely in that big house," I said, watching a big white bird swoop overhead and land near the sidewalk.

"Yeah," Nikki said, looking a little perplexed. "I guess it could." She said it like she didn't think my aunt was lonely.

"What do you mean?" I asked.

"Order up," the cook called out.

Nikki grabbed my order and bagged it.

"Here you go," she said, handing over my bag and soda. "Enjoy your lunch."

I thanked her and went to sit at one of the tables to eat.

A chipmunk darted out, stood up on his hind legs and begged.

"I'm probably not supposed to feed you," I told him, then tossed him a bite of tortilla which he grabbed and ran away with.

It was noticeably quiet without the roar of cars and other normal city sounds. It was so quiet I could hear the gentle lapping of the water against the shore.

Two boys raced past on their bicycles.

I wondered why Nikki had seemed surprised that I thought my aunt was lonely in the big house. It was a big house. It had the guest bedroom downstairs. Four bedrooms upstairs, one used as an office. The upstairs was set up so that there was even a small kitchenette. Just a refrigerator, microwave, and sink.

When I was upstairs, I felt like I was in a whole different house than downstairs. I rarely even went into the downstairs kitchen except to make morning coffee.

Nikki probably hadn't meant anything by it. Sometimes I got a little confused by the northern mid-western accent. I'm sure they were confused by my Dallas accent, too.

Chapter 4
Cody

WHEN I LANDED at the Mackinac runway—there was no actual airport on the island—there was a cargo wagon waiting for me.

Betty would have set that up. She had set everything up, including the room I would be living out of for the next six months.

I had all the information in my phone, but turned out I didn't need any of it. The driver already knew everything, even the address.

The sun was bright, overhead now, but away from the runway itself, it was cool in the shade of the trees.

I'd been to Mackinac Island before, but only to drop off or pick up. I had never spent any time here and had never toured the anything other than what I could see from the sky.

With six months, I would have time to see everything, including the Grand Hotel and the old fort.

Betty, who knew everything about all Skye Travels activity, said an average of one flight a week out was chartered. I was going to have lots of time to explore in between charters.

Since Mike was married with one child and about to have two, it was the perfect schedule for him, giving him lots of time for family.

I think I would go stir crazy living here.

I had to admit, though, as I climbed up on the front of the wagon, and we started down the road toward town, there was a certain charm to the island.

There were only two ways on and off the island. Boat and airplane. There was no bridge to drive over to get here. I found it fascinating that there were houses of all sizes here including the Grand Hotel. The Grand Hotel where *Somewhere in Time* had been filmed carried the distinction of having the longest porch in the world.

We traveled through downtown, an area populated with tourists, then kept going, traveling along the shoreline now.

As we left town, the only sound was the steady clip-clop of the horses' hooves and the mournful wail of the ferry's horn out on the water.

From here the lake looked like an ocean.

Outside of town, the houses along the shore as Main Street turned into Lakeshore Blvd were called cottages, but they looked more like historical Victorian and Gothic style mansions to me. The lawns were well-manicured and all had pink and yellow flowers giving them pops of color.

The driver stopped at one of those Victorian mansions, a cute house with lots of roof cuts in its three-stories. The house was a light gray, a color that matched the sky on a stormy afternoon. And my, it had windows.

"This is it," the driver said.

"Are you sure?" I asked, checking the address on my phone.

The driver laughed. "What were you expecting?"

I ran a hand along my chin and shook my hand. "I don't even know, but it wasn't this."

"Let's get you unloaded, shall we?" he asked.

"Yes." I hopped off the wagon. What had I been expecting? Certainly not a high-rise. Maybe I had been expecting more of a cabin.

Whatever it was, I decided, it would be an adventure.

Chapter 5
Bailey

I TOOK my time getting home, walking along the shore, enjoying the soothing lapping of water against the shore. Birds gliding in the wind.

I waved at one of the neighbors out working in her front yard.

It was just so unbelievably peaceful here. When I had been a teenager, I had been too interested in friends and boys, boys mostly, to appreciate it here.

But now, ten years later, I had come a long way. I stopped and sat on one of the benches to watch a ferry as it left the docks, taking people toward the mainland.

I'd learned that there were ferries for tourists and there were boats that residents could charter to take them to the mainland for things like shopping, doctors, anything really.

Once on the mainland, they could rent a car and go wherever they wanted.

The chartered boats were a lot more affordable than taking a private jet, but there were plenty of those coming and going, too.

I wondered how my aunt traveled. By ferry or boat or plane. I'd come in by ferry when I visited and the two of us didn't travel anywhere other than around the island while I was here.

There was so much I didn't know about her and yet she had left this house to me. I'd done a little research and learned that houses on Mackinac Island, like the one she left me in her will weren't easy to qualify for.

I was becoming rather attached to living here. At twenty-six, I would probably be the youngest single person living here alone, at least on purpose. I hadn't exactly done a survey, so I could be wrong. My neighbor with the Siberian husky lived alone, but he was more my aunt's age.

My extended lunch break over, I headed back to the house. I could get in a few hours of work before sunset. Watching the sun set was my next scheduled break time.

I reached the sidewalk leading to my front door—none of the houses had driveways—and turned right following the walkway.

About halfway down, surrounded by the sweet scent of magnolia blossoms, I stopped, my feet frozen to the sidewalk.

There was a man sitting on the steps of the front porch, his head down, looking at his phone. He was surrounded by three suitcases, a red bicycle, and a golf bag.

What the—?

My thoughts raced through possibilities. Another relative. Someone at the wrong house?

Then I remembered my conversation with Betty. I hadn't

forgotten about it—it was too much money to forget about, but I wasn't thinking about it right now.

It had been so long, I'd actually been waiting for her to ask for her money back.

But… this could be the boarder she had sent.

She hadn't given me a name. I guess it slipped her mind.

Or maybe I hadn't answered the landline.

I started walking forward again, words of welcome on my lips.

But then he looked up.

And every cell in my body stopped functioning.

This was not possible.

But when he stood up and smiled at me, I knew it was.

Cody Johnson was my boarder.

Keep Reading SEALED WITH A KISS…

Kathryn Kaleigh writes sweet romantic comedy, time travel romance, and historical romance.

kathrynkaleigh.com

www.ingramcontent.com/pod-product-compliance
Lightning Source LLC
Chambersburg PA
CBHW020148120726
47903CB00007B/2463